Hannah smiled, and Ross felt his blood pressure go up a few degrees— from the smile, and from the worn, oversize T-shirt she was wearing.

The soft cotton molded her breasts with loving faithfulness, something she didn't seem to realize. Nor did she seem to realize there were worn places in the fabric that made it damn near transparent.

Don't stare, he reminded himself.

A gentleman would keep his eyes directed elsewhere. More importantly, he didn't want to find Hannah attractive, not in that way. He didn't trust his judgment when love and sex were involved.

A marriage based on friendship was a much safer bet. Hannah might not be his type romantically, but she was definitely a friend. They could be together, just like when they were kids.

"So…" he said slowly, "how about marrying me?"

Bridal Fever:

Three partners find their bachelor days numbered when the Alaskan nights get long and lonely….

BRIDAL FEVER!

Callie, Get Your Groom (SR#1436)
Hannah Gets a Husband (SR#1448)
Jodie's Mail-Order Man (SR#1460)

Dear Reader,

♪♫"Happy Birthday to us...."♪♫ Exactly twenty years ago this May, Silhouette Romance was born. Since then, we've grown as a company, and as a series that continues to offer the very best in contemporary category romance fiction. The icing on the cake is this month's amazing lineup:

International bestselling author Diana Palmer reprises her SOLDIERS OF FORTUNE miniseries with *Mercenary's Woman.* Sorely missed, Rita Rainville returns to Romance with the delightful story of a *Too Hard To Handle* rancher who turns out to be anything but.... Elizabeth August delivers the dramatic finale to ROYALLY WED. In *A Royal Mission,* rescuing kidnapped missing princess Victoria Rockford was easy for Lance Grayson. But falling in love wasn't part of the plan.

Marie Ferrarella charms us with a *Tall, Strong & Cool Under Fire* hero whose world turns topsy-turvy when an adorable moppet and her enticing mom venture into his fire station.... Julianna Morris's BRIDAL FEVER! rages on when *Hannah Gets a Husband*—her childhood friend who is a new dad. And in *Her Sister's Child,* a woman allies with her enemy. Don't miss this pulse-pounding romance by Lilian Darcy!

In June, we're featuring Dixie Browning and Phyllis Halldorson, and in coming months look for new miniseries from many of your favorite authors. It's an exciting year for Silhouette Books, and we invite you to join the celebration!

Happy reading!

Mary-Theresa Hussey

Mary-Theresa Hussey
Senior Editor

Please address questions and book requests to:
Silhouette Reader Service
U.S.: 3010 Walden Ave., P.O. Box 1325, Buffalo, NY 14269
Canadian: P.O. Box 609, Fort Erie, Ont. L2A 5X3

HANNAH GETS A HUSBAND

Julianna Morris

Silhouette
R O M A N C E™
Published by Silhouette Books
America's Publisher of Contemporary Romance

To all my friends in Tulare

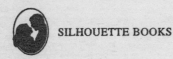 SILHOUETTE BOOKS

ISBN 0-373-19448-X

HANNAH GETS A HUSBAND

Visit Silhouette at www.eHarlequin.com

Printed in U.S.A.

JULIANNA MORRIS

has an offbeat sense of humor, which frequently gets her into trouble. She is often accused of being curious about everything…her interests ranging from oceanography and photography to traveling, antiquing, walking on the beach and reading science fiction. Choosing a college major was extremely difficult, but after many changes she earned a bachelor's degree in environmental science.

Julianna's writing is supervised by a cat named Gandalf, who sits on the computer monitor and criticizes each keystroke. Ultimately, she would like a home overlooking the ocean, where she can write to her heart's content—and Gandalf's malcontent. She'd like to share that home with her own romantic hero, someone with a warm, sexy smile, lots of patience and an offbeat sense of humor to match her own. Oh, yes…and he has to like cats.

IT'S OUR 20th ANNIVERSARY!
We'll be celebrating all year,
Continuing with these fabulous titles,
On sale in May 2000.

Romance

 #1444 Mercenary's Woman
Diana Palmer

#1445 Too Hard To Handle
Rita Rainville

 #1446 A Royal Mission
Elizabeth August

#1447 Tall, Strong & Cool Under Fire
Marie Ferrarella

 #1448 Hannah Gets a Husband
Julianna Morris

#1449 Her Sister's Child
Lilian Darcy

Desire

 #1291 Dr. Irresistible
Elizabeth Bevarly

 #1292 Expecting His Child
Leanne Banks

#1293 In His Loving Arms
Cindy Gerard

 #1294 Sheikh's Honor
Alexandra Sellers

 #1295 The Baby Bonus
Metsy Hingle

#1296 Did You Say Married?!
Kathie DeNosky

Intimate Moments

 #1003 Rogue's Reform
Marilyn Pappano

 #1004 The Cowboy's Hidden Agenda
Kathleen Creighton

#1005 In a Heartbeat
Carla Cassidy

 #1006 Anything for Her Marriage
Karen Templeton

#1007 Every Little Thing
Linda Winstead Jones

 #1008 Remember the Night
Linda Castillo

Special Edition

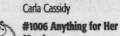 **#1321 The Kincaid Bride**
Jackie Merritt

 #1322 The Millionaire She Married
Christine Rimmer

#1323 Warrior's Embrace
Peggy Webb

 #1324 The Sheik's Arranged Marriage
Susan Mallery

#1325 Sullivan's Child
Gail Link

#1326 Wild Mustang
Jane Toombs

Chapter One

Bong, bong, bong.

The bell in the tiny church tower rang three times, announcing the end of the wedding ceremony.

Hannah Liggett leaned her elbows on the cash register and sighed. Those bongs meant it was official—she was the last single woman in Quicksilver, Alaska.

Single, as in spinster.

Ten Penny Alice was marrying Joe Dobkins—bride and groom were both in their nineties. Hannah didn't know how Ten Penny had gotten her name, but she suspected it had something to do with the bawdy house Ten Penny once owned.

"I wonder if the bride wore white?" Hannah mused aloud, an aching sensation tugging at her heart. It wasn't envy, but she couldn't help wondering if she'd ever fall in love and get married herself. Of course, she'd been too busy raising her brothers to look for a husband, but that didn't mean she'd stopped thinking about it.

"Don't feel s'bad," called Toby Myers, one of the old sourdoughs who always hung around the restaurant. "I'll marry up with ya."

Hannah lifted the coffeepot and walked to his table. "I don't know about that. You know what they say about getting married in Alaska...the odds are good, but the goods are odd."

He chuckled as she poured another cup of coffee. It wasn't the strong stuff he really wanted—Toby's doctor had ordered *absolutely no caffeine,* so she was secretly substituting decaf. So far, he hadn't noticed the difference.

The bell over the door jangled and Hannah glanced up, surprised. She didn't expect the guests to arrive for another few minutes; when the bride and groom were ninety-two and ninety-five respectively, it took a while to get places.

"Hi, Hannah. Remember me?" a man asked, shifting the child he held in his arms.

Hannah stepped closer so the newcomer wasn't silhouetted against the late-afternoon light. Her eyes opened wider.

It was Ross McCoy, but not the lanky teenager who'd left Quicksilver nearly seventeen years ago. *This* Ross was six foot two, with broad shoulders and a trim, powerful body that oozed masculine sensuality. *Potent.* Small lines fanned the corners of his deep blue eyes, topped by black hair with a few glints of silver.

Shocked by the feminine awareness running through her body, she stared at the child he carried, then at Ross again. They had the same hair and eyes, the same strong chin and direct way of looking at you. They looked so much alike there was no doubt they were father and son.

"Have I changed that much?" Ross murmured.

"Ross?" Hannah whispered.

"Yup." He grinned his slow, warm grin. "Well, Honeycomb? Where's that hug you always used to give me?"

The familiar nickname and smile made Hannah's eyes swim with unaccustomed tears. "I...uh...." She shrugged and sniffed in embarrassment.

Ross put his son down on a chair and closed the distance between them. He lifted his hand and stroked a damp track on her cheek. "Hey, what's all this? You don't cry."

"Nothing. I'm just glad to see you."

"Same here, Honeycomb."

He gave her a quick, tight hug and Hannah drew an unsteady breath. Some things might have changed, but she was still "Honeycomb" to Ross, the nickname he'd given her when they'd gleefully found an old tree filled with bees and honey, only to be chased away by a territorial bear.

It was just like him to show up when she was a little lost and at odds with herself during this wedding excitement. Despite the years she'd spent riding herd on six younger brothers, she still dreamed of becoming a mother. Of course, that required a husband, and men didn't seem to find her particularly desirable.

Jeez, that was depressing—even more depressing than never having a family of her own. Most of the time Hannah tried not to think about the lack of romance in her life, but the fuss over Ten Penny finally getting married was a constant reminder.

"Think I'll be headin' out," said Toby.

Hannah blinked and motioned to the pink streamers

adorning the room. "Aren't you staying for the party, Toby? There's lots of food."

"Nope...gotta get going. I'm organizin' the chivaree for Joe and Ten Penny, so I need to get ever'thing fixed up for it." The door closed behind him, leaving an overwhelming silence.

Ross lifted his eyebrows. "A chivaree?"

Hannah tucked an errant strand of hair behind her ear and shrugged again. Ordinarily she didn't pay much attention to her appearance, yet this was one day she wished she could have worn something besides her usual jeans and shirt. The last time Ross had seen her, she'd been a flat-chested fifteen-year-old, trying to make her youngest brother eat green peas without spitting them in her hair. Maybe she didn't have any illusions about being beautiful, but it would have been nice to look her best.

"You probably don't remember," she murmured. "It's an old custom. The men 'serenade' the bride and groom on their wedding night, making noise and keeping them from...er, getting amorous."

"I remember, but Joe and Ten Penny are pretty old for that sort of thing."

"It's all in fun, and Ten Penny has been hankering after a chivaree for a long time," Hannah said, remembering how excited the elder woman had been about her impending nuptials.

"Hmm...I didn't think she was the romantic type."

Every woman is the romantic type, you dope, Hannah thought, unaccountably annoyed. Yet it really wasn't Ross's fault. Everyone in town had teased her about being the last spinster in Quicksilver, thinking she was too practical, too *sensible* to mind the good-natured ribbing. Sometimes it felt like Sensible Hannah was tattooed across her forehead.

Sensible. *Hah.*

Pressing her lips together, she hurried to Toby's table to clean it up before the wedding guests arrived, mostly to give herself something to do. She wanted to ask about the little boy Ross had brought with him, but figured Ross would explain in his own good time.

Crouching to retrieve a dropped spoon, she caught the child's eye and smiled. The youngster regarded her gravely, then scooted off his chair to tug on his father's pant leg. The ache around Hannah's heart deepened. Everyone had moved on with their lives, and here she was, in the same old place she'd always been.

"Up, Papa."

"All right, Jamie."

Ross bent and lifted his son into his arms again. He'd fought so hard to get custody of Jamie, sometimes he was afraid to let go.

Jamie put his thumb in his mouth and stared at Hannah. Ross didn't blame him, he could hardly keep from staring himself. She'd changed...*a lot.* He remembered a girl with a flyaway blond hair and a gamin face, but that girl had turned into a woman with expressive silver-green eyes and a shapely body.

Very shapely.

Get a grip, Ross ordered, trying to quell a flash of heat in his groin. That wasn't why he'd returned to Quicksilver. He'd returned because Hannah was a good friend and he needed her help. When it came right down to it, she was the only woman he really trusted.

Woman. He grinned at the thought.

Hannah hadn't *quite* been a woman when he'd left

Quicksilver, but it didn't matter; they'd gotten into too much trouble together to ever be strangers. Hours of writing "I'll never build a snowman on the teacher's chair again" were a guarantee of lifelong friendship.

"What are you smirking about?" Hannah asked.

"Our infamous snowman. How many times did we have to write that sentence?"

"A thousand times each. My hand developed a permanent crimp, and it was all your idea to do it."

Ross shook his head. "Not quite. You were the one who suggested we dye the snow green and use a witch's cap. That was the part Mrs. Haggerty hated the worst."

"All right, we were both responsible." Hannah laughed, her cheeks turning pink. He loved it; she was probably the only woman left on the planet unspoiled enough to blush.

After his disastrous marriage he'd vowed never to be trapped again, but getting Jamie had changed everything. He needed a wife to strengthen his legal position in case of another custody battle, and his son needed a mother. Hannah was the solution to both problems.

He'd thought it out very carefully. Hannah had grown up in Alaska and she was great with kids. And she was the loyal type—at just fourteen she'd taken over caring for the family when her mother died in childbirth. He knew she'd marry him if she understood how important it was; they'd always stuck together.

Hannah came closer, her attention focused on Jamie. "Hello. My name is Hannah. Who are you?"

"Jamie. I'm four." He held up all five of his fingers.

She tucked his thumb down, then touched the remaining fingers one by one. "This many is four. One, two, three, four. See?"

He regarded his hand for a solemn second. In fact, he was entirely too solemn and grave for a child his age, something that could be blamed on his flighty mother. Ross's mouth tightened with determination; Jamie deserved to have Hannah as his mother, and that's exactly what his son was going to get.

"Okay," Jamie agreed. "Can I have some ice cream?"

"May I," Ross corrected.

Jamie sighed heavily. "Okay. Can Papa have some, too?"

An exasperated expression crossed his father's face, but Hannah smiled. After raising six brothers, she could handle little boys. A sense of humor helped, along with a huge tolerance for noise and cheerful chaos.

"Of course he can have some ice cream. I know your papa likes strawberry the best, but what's your favorite?"

"V'nilla." Jamie leaned forward and held out his arms. With an ease born of long practice, Hannah shifted the youngster onto her hip.

"I need to talk to you, Hannah," said Ross, following them to a corner table. "It's important."

For some reason her stomach fluttered, though she couldn't imagine why. They'd talked about everything when they were kids; why should it be different now? The fact that Ross had turned into a heart-stopping hunk didn't mean anything.

And don't forget Jamie.

Right.

Little boys had mothers, which meant there was a

good chance Ross was married. So it would be silly to be attracted to an old friend, and even sillier to imagine he was attracted to her. It was just this wedding stuff, getting her stirred up and confused. Just the same, it would be nice to have someone really want her.

"Hannah?"

"Uhh...all right. Except I'd better get that ice cream first. Isn't that right, Jamie? A nice big bowl."

Jamie's eyes brightened. "V'nilla."

"And strawberry for your papa. We'll be right back, Ross."

Ross sat back and watched Hannah disappear into the restaurant kitchen with his son. "I heard Deke is working on a fishing boat," he called. "He's the youngest, isn't he?"

"Yes." Her voice was muffled. "He took off a couple of months ago to earn money for college. Deke is just like you. He couldn't wait to get away."

Ross shifted in the old ladder-back chair. Yeah, he'd been anxious to leave Quicksilver. It was a dusty little town, forgotten by the modern world and lumbering toward extinction. The principal entertainments were hunting, drinking and watching moss grow on trees.

On the other hand, Hannah had never seemed to mind living in Quicksilver. She'd listened patiently when he talked about escaping, but her family was the center of her world, not exotic travel and different places. And he had to admit, if he'd been part of the Liggett clan he might have felt the same. They weren't perfect, but they were nice people.

"Here we go," Hannah said a moment later. She held a tray in one hand and led Jamie with the other.

"Thanks." Ross settled his son on his lap and

tucked a napkin under his chin. It was awkward. Jamie had only been living with him for a few weeks and they were still adjusting to each other.

Just then the sound of excited, happy people floated into the restaurant and Hannah grinned. "That's the wedding party coming over from the church."

"I couldn't believe it when your dad said Ten Penny was getting married."

She gave him a strange look. "When did you talk to my father?"

"A few days ago."

Hannah straightened, still watching Ross with a question in her eyes. She didn't like hearing that he'd talked to her dad, especially since her father had been walking around all week like a cat who'd stolen the cream. Anyway, if Ross had something to talk to her about, why wouldn't he call her directly?

"Danged if this isn't something," cried Ten Penny as she tottered through the door. "I'm finally a missus!" Everyone else was dressed in the usual jeans and shirts, but Ten Penny wore a purple feather boa around her neck and a beaded dress of unknown vintage.

"Congratulations, *Mrs.* Dobkins," Hannah said, giving Ten Penny a hug. "You look beautiful." And she meant it. Maybe Ten Penny had a few wrinkles and a questionable reputation in the murky past, but none of that mattered today. She was beautiful…a survivor, a monument to stubborn determination in the face of great odds.

"You sure made it all look purty in here," said Ten Penny. "All them flowers and ribbons and such. It's a real weddin' party. Thanks, darlin'."

"I enjoyed doing it," Hannah assured her. "Now go sit down and have a good time."

The combination bar and restaurant wasn't very big, and with half the town crowded inside, the noise level skyrocketed. In the distant past Ten Penny had heard about "petit fours" and "little sandwiches without crusts," so she'd asked Hannah to make some of those "fancy goo-gaws" for her big day. Fortunately Hannah had also made red-hot chili and several sheet cakes—Quicksilver wasn't ready for finger food.

When she got the chance, Hannah pulled her father to one side. "What's going on with Ross McCoy? You never said anything about talking to him."

"Oh? You know he calls the bar every now and then—more before his pa died, of course. The McCoys never had a phone. He always asks about you, too."

Hannah ignored the pleasure her father's last statement gave her. "Yes, but why is he here?"

"You'll have to ask Ross. My, that chocolate cake looks good. I'd better get over there before it's all gone."

"Wily old fox," Hannah muttered.

"Whatever you say, dear. By the way, did I mention Ross is divorced?"

With that last remark, Edgar Liggett made a beeline for the food table, leaving Hannah with narrowed eyes and a tapping foot. She loved her father, but he had an annoying ability to duck out of uncomfortable situations.

And what did he mean about Ross being divorced? With Edgar it could be anything from idle conversation to a suggestion she seduce the guy. Hannah froze at the thought, then shook her head. The idea had a certain appeal, but she didn't have any skills in the seduction department and she wouldn't want to hurt her friendship with Ross, anyway. It was funny, but even after all these years, she still considered him her best friend. If her life had gone a little differently, they might have kept in touch. He'd done better than she had—at least he'd written her a few letters.

As for what Ross wanted…she didn't know what to think. He sat in the corner, calmly eating ice cream with his son and chatting with the partygoers as though he'd never left Quicksilver. Feeling foolish, Hannah headed over to his table on the pretext of bringing Jamie a glass of milk.

"Thanks." Ross smiled and motioned to the chair next to him. "Can you take a break?"

"Sure. You wanted to talk, didn't you?"

"Yeah." He pushed the last of his ice cream away. "I understand you never got married."

"Thanks, rub it in," Hannah muttered.

He looked surprised. "I didn't mean anything."

"Of course not."

No longer curious, she grabbed his bowl and headed for the kitchen. So much for thinking Ross might understand how she felt. It was different for men; they could father babies until they were old and gray. They didn't have to worry about biological clocks, which probably explained why they didn't obsess about falling in love nearly so much as the female half of the species.

"Hannah…"

"What?" she asked.

"I didn't mean to upset you."

Hannah sighed. She was being overly sensitive, but that didn't change the way she felt. "Forget it." But he stood there waiting and she shrugged. "It's just that

I've been teased a lot about Ten Penny's wedding—you know, about it making me the last spinster. I thought you were getting into the fun, as well.''

Genuine shock registered on his face. ''I'd never do that, Hannah. I only brought it up because—''

''Honey, that punch could use some more kick,'' called Ten Penny into the kitchen. ''But yer daddy's fresh out of gin at the bar and he can't find his keys to the storeroom.''

Hannah leaned her forehead against the worn wood of a cabinet for a second. *A kick.* That's all she needed—a bunch of elderly revelers getting punch drunk. ''Okay, I'll get it.''

She hurried out again, at the same time checking on Jamie. Despite her muddled emotions, Hannah smiled. Ross had left the boy with three older women, who clucked over him like a bunch of broody hens. There weren't many children in Quicksilver; the town didn't have any opportunities for young families, so most of them migrated to larger communities like Anchorage or Fairbanks.

Ross caught her arm. ''Let's sneak out for a little while.''

''I'm busy.'' Hannah pulled away, but he followed her to the storeroom. *Honestly,* he'd waited over seventeen years to come see her, and now he acted like the building was on fire and he didn't have a moment to waste.

''I am very, very serious. Could we please go somewhere private?'' he asked.

Hannah rolled her eyes. ''I have a wedding reception to take care of, Ross. Why don't you roll up your sleeves and help me? There's plenty of time. We can talk later.''

"Well, I—"

"Honey, where's that gin?" call Ten Penny.

"Coming."

Sighing again, Hannah hunted up a bottle and pushed past Ross. The small room felt even smaller with him filling up the entrance, his eyes dark and intent as they watched her. It was uncomfortable, feeling so aware of him as a man.

"Here you go."

She handed the bottle to Ten Penny, who proceeded to empty it into the bowl. Hannah grimaced as the scent of gin assailed her senses; ordinarily she left serving spirits to her father, but this was a special occasion.

"That's better, darlin'," said Ten Penny, smacking her lips over the fortified punch. She handed a cup to her groom, who nodded with equal approval.

"That's fine," Joe crowed. "Have some, too, Hannah girl. "It'll put hair on yer chest."

His bride shook a finger at him. "Hush, Joe. Hannah don't need no hair on her chest. Ain't that right, Ross?" she called. "You been looking plenty at Hannah's chest. It looks just dandy, don't it?"

"Uh…" Ross choked, and heat crept up his neck. "Her chest is fine."

Edgar Liggett stood across the room, glaring with parental indignation, and Ross whistled beneath his breath. Proposing to Hannah was a whole lot more complicated than he'd thought it would be. As for Hannah… He turned and saw her studying him with a strained expression on her face.

Great. Thanks to Joe and Ten Penny she probably thought he'd turned into a sex fiend over the years, and it wasn't true. He was a normal man who enjoyed looking at a woman's body; Hannah had grown up very nicely and he appreciated that fact.

"Hannah?" called someone else from across the room. "You got any more coffee?"

"And sugar," added another voice.

Ross gritted his teeth. It seemed as if everyone in Quicksilver had a claim on Hannah's time and attention, and a vague sense of guilt nagged at him. Was he being fair, hoping to get her sympathy with Jamie? Or would she be grateful for the chance to finally get away from Quicksilver?

His frustration built as he kept trying to get her alone. "Sit down," he said when she scooted past him for the seventh time.

She gave him a distracted smile. "After a bit."

It was the last straw. "Hannah Liggett," he roared. "I want to propose! So, will you or won't you marry me?" Ross regretted the words as soon as they left his mouth, but it was too late and he was too frazzled to care.

Except for an excited titter next to the food table, the room fell silent.

Hannah turned white and stared at him. "What?"

He loosened the collar around his neck. "I...uh, asked you to marry me."

"That's what I thought." Turning, she headed straight for the door of the restaurant. Ross thought there were tears in her eyes and he swore under his breath.

"Watch Jamie for a minute, okay?" he asked Hannah's father before heading out the door himself.

If there was one thing he hated, it was seeing Hannah cry. She'd always been so brave when they were growing up, taking her lumps and smiling through everything. There was only one other time he'd seen her really crying, and he still remembered the horrid feeling it gave him.

More from instinct than memory, he found her in the small copse of trees where she'd always gone to be alone. Ross sighed at the sight of her standing there, her hands clenched into fists.

"Ah, Hannah. I didn't mean to upset you."

Her chin lifted and he saw she wasn't upset—she was furious. "How could you say something like that in front of everyone? Do you enjoy making a fool out of me?"

"But I *do* want to marry you."

Hannah wanted to kick him. He didn't get it at *all*. It couldn't have been more obvious to the entire town that Ross didn't have any romantic feelings for her. They were probably having a rib-splitting chuckle over the whole thing.

"Jamie needs a mother," Ross continued quietly. "And you're the only woman I could ever trust him with."

She ground her teeth. Ross wanted to marry reliable old Hannah—cook, baby-sitter and all-around good sport. She'd moaned about being the last single woman in Quicksilver, but this wasn't what she'd had in mind to correct the matter. Jeez, she felt so stupid for getting worked up about Ross; he didn't have any interest in her, not as a woman.

"You should wait to fall in love," she muttered. "That'll be best for Jamie."

Ross studied her, his hands thrust in his pockets. "I was in love with my first wife and it was a disaster. But this would be great—two friends getting married. Don't you see how perfect it is? We always backed each other up when things got bad. And friendship is a much better basis for marriage than some fleeting emotion based mostly on lust.''

Hannah wanted to scream ''no.'' No she wouldn't marry him. And no, love meant more than just lust. Yet she couldn't help remembering Jamie's solemn, almost worried face; her pride wasn't the only thing to consider. And Ross obviously valued their friendship, so it wasn't like he didn't care about her. In a way he'd paid her a huge compliment.

''Maybe I could be your housekeeper,'' she suggested.

''No.'' Ross shook his head. ''My ex-wife signed over custody for a large monetary settlement, but she's already making noises about getting Jamie back. I need a wife and a stable family life so any judge in the world will agree that Jamie belongs in Alaska with me. And I need to do it fast, Honeycomb...before she has a chance to file any papers with the court. It'll look better.''

''I don't understand,'' Hannah murmured, still getting a rush of pleasure that he remembered her old nickname. ''If she signed over custody, then how can she do anything?''

He sighed heavily. ''According to my lawyer, when it comes to kids and the legal system, you never know what could happen. Besides, Jamie needs to feel secure. I want him to have a real mother.''

Hannah pressed her hand to her throat, feeling the familiar, longing ache. *A real mother.*

She loved her brothers, but she wasn't their mother; now Ross was offering her a dream come true. It had felt so right, talking to Jamie and holding him...and it wasn't like men were hanging around, begging her to marry them. This could be her last chance. Should she settle for part of what she wanted, rather than risk not getting anything at all?

But marrying Ross? Hannah swallowed.

Just how married did he expect them to be? Married as in *really* married, or married as in separate bedrooms? She peeked at him from beneath her lashes, but didn't know how to ask. Of course, she doubted he expected anything physical. They were friends, not lovers. He'd made that very clear.

"So...for how long were you thinking we'd be married? A year or two?"

"At least till Jamie is eighteen," he said decisively. "He needs someone he knows will always be there for him. And you never know, we might really like it. I could see us staying together, can't you?"

Oh, sure, Hannah thought wryly. A nice platonic little marriage—every woman's lifelong dream.

"Think about it," Ross urged. "I know I should have handled things differently, but this is your chance to leave Quicksilver. We'd live down on the Kenai Peninsula, but you could go to Anchorage whenever you like. I'm a partner in an air transit business—I can give you a good life."

Once again Hannah's foot itched to kick him. Honestly, the man had developed a genuine talent for making her angry. Not that it was anything new. They may have been buddies, but they'd fought like cats and dogs when they were kids. Why should anything be different now?

"My big chance, huh? Do you think I'd marry you for that?"

He sighed. "Of course not. I just wanted to reassure you that...well, that I'm—"

"A good provider?" she asked, a little too sweetly.

"If you want to put it that way. I couldn't blame you for wondering what you'd get out of the arrangement."

Get out of the arrangement?

All at once Hannah realized there was a part of Ross she no longer knew...the part that had gotten cynical. More confused than ever, she stared at the Sitka spruce trees surrounding them. A long time ago Ross had found her here, crying after her mother's funeral. He'd held her and comforted her, though he'd hardly said a word.

Where was *that* Ross? The tall, strong boy who understood her grief more than anyone else? She might have been comfortable marrying the boy she'd once known, but he'd gone and turned into a sexy hunk who didn't believe in love.

"Please...I didn't mean to hurt you, Hannah. You're very special to me. You always have been."

She tapped her fingers on her arm. "I suppose you thought I'd be thrilled to get a proposal from *anyone*."

Ross winced, realizing how badly he'd handled things. How could he make her understand? When he'd finally gotten Jamie and realized his son needed a mother as well as a father, the woman he'd instantly thought of was Hannah Liggett.

Hell, as far as he was concerned, there *wasn't* any other choice. Hannah was sweet and generous and loyal to a fault with her friends and family. She was the perfect mother for his son. And to be honest, having her in his life again wouldn't be bad for him, either.

"I wasn't implying anything of the sort," he said, carefully picking his words.

"Cut it out," Hannah snapped. "You claim you didn't mean to embarrass me, but what did you expect? Everyone knows we haven't been seeing each other. I'll bet they're still laughing at the grand joke."

"Marrying me isn't a joke."

"It is when you're the last single woman in town. It is when the proposal is yelled out during a wedding reception where the ninety-two-year-old bride managed to get a husband ahead of you!"

Ross groaned. No wonder Hannah wanted to crown him; in her shoes he would have been furious too.

"Look, Hannah, I think you're terrific—that's why I'm here. I'll tell everyone I've always been in love with you, and that I got carried away by the moment. I can be very convincing. Heck, they're halfway convinced already—when Ten Penny said that stuff about me looking at your chest, your father looked like he wanted to geld me with a kitchen knife."

Hannah narrowed her eyes. Bringing up the comments about her "chest" wasn't something she appreciated. He'd described her chest as "fine." Fine was one of those words like "interesting." You said it when you didn't know what else to say.

Fine.

Yuck.

"Huh. Trust me, Dad isn't the protective type. Please, just go away and leave me alone. I need to think."

"*No.*" He barked the order out and Hannah glared.

"I can be alone if I want. We're not married yet…and I doubt we'll ever *be* married," she added darkly.

"Don't say that. I sincerely, abjectly apologize for embarrassing you."

"Stow it." Hannah stepped back and abruptly went flying, her foot caught in a rabbit hole. A stab of pain shot through her ankle as she hit the ground.

"Hannah! Are you okay? No, stay down. Let me check you first."

Ross's hand held her gently in place, when all she wanted was to crawl in that dratted hole. A woman could only take so much humiliation in one day, and she'd reached her absolute limit.

"I'm all right. Leave me alone."

Ignoring the protest, he slid his fingers over her ribs, leaving a trail of heat that made it even harder to breathe. His knuckles lightly brushed the underside of her breasts and Hannah's heart lodged in her throat.

Lord, it wasn't fair.

Ross was practically caressing her and he looked about as stimulated as a sleeping walrus. The tumble hadn't done her any serious physical damage, but at the moment, her feminine ego was on the critical list.

Chapter Two

"Does this hurt?" Ross asked, probing down her leg.

A breath hissed out between Hannah's teeth. She felt awfully funny...kind of hot and tingly in some very private places. "Really, I'm fine," she assured him. "You don't have to do this."

Typically male, he ignored her, moving on to the other leg. When he reached her ankle and lifted it, she flinched, unable to hide a twinge of pain.

"Oh, you're fine, all right," he muttered.

Hannah stuck her tongue out at Ross's bent head. Know-it-all. So what if she'd gotten hurt? It wasn't any concern of his. "Don't fuss. It's just a slight sprain."

He slipped her shoe off to examine the injury, supporting her leg on his thigh. His strong fingers circled her foot and Hannah bit her lip to keep from making a sound.

She'd read about sexual attraction, of course, but

she'd never felt anything like this before today. A few shots of quickening pulse and sighs were the extent of her experience; if anything, she'd assumed her sex drive was virtually nonexistent.

But noooo.

Along comes Ross McCoy, fully grown, to prove she's no different than all the other hormone-driven women on the planet.

Drat Ross anyway.

What business did he have coming back here and making her react this way? It had to be that mid-thirties sexual peak thing, starting a couple years early.

"I don't see any swelling," he said finally. "But I'd better carry you back, just in case."

"That isn't necessary," Hannah returned hastily. She could just imagine the whispers and smirks if she got carried back into town after running out of the restaurant in a huff.

"Of course it's necessary." Ross turned his head and grinned at her. "Besides, think how gallant and romantic it'll look. Everyone will be convinced I'm crazy about you. By the way, start thinking whether you want to get married in Anchorage, or here in Quicksilver."

Arrogant wretch.

Hannah glowered; he just assumed she'd fall in with his plans and marry him. "We're not getting married, Ross," she said, jerking her foot away from his grasp. "I am not that desperate for a husband."

"Boy, talk about insulting," he returned good-naturedly. "Are you saying a woman would have to be really *really* desperate to marry me?"

"Listen to me." She tapped her finger on his chest for emphasis. "I may not be gorgeous or well traveled, but you can't order me around. Look somewhere else for your convenient wife.''

Ross blinked, astonished. "You're very pretty, Hannah. Don't you know that?''

"Whatever. But you're not listening to me.''

"I *am* listening." Ross captured Hannah's face between his hands and gazed intently into her eyes; this was one battle he intended to win. "I fought too hard for Jamie to give up now. Doreen walked out when she was two months pregnant, and it's been nothing but hell since then. It was over a year before I could even see my son.''

Idly Ross noticed Hannah's eyes had turned the deep, turbulent color of a storm, all traces of green erased by inner turmoil. He was making a shameless play for her sympathy, but he'd deal with his conscience later. Right now he had to convince her.

"Honeycomb, if anyone is desperate, it's me," he whispered urgently. "Jamie has nightmares and he's withdrawn. You can help him—I could tell right off by the way he took to you.''

"I'll…think about it," Hannah said slowly.

A rush of adrenaline made him want to push, *make* her say yes. Yet he hadn't helped build a successful business by driving a deal too hard and fast. He'd just stay in Quicksilver for as long as it took. With Hannah's soft heart, it shouldn't take more than a couple of days to make her relent. And she couldn't avoid him, not in such a small town.

"Okay, I'll take you back to the restaurant.''

She gasped and clutched an arm around his neck when he swung her into his arms. "Ross, I'm too heavy. Put me down.''

"Heavy?" He shook his head in amazement. "You

have the oddest ideas about yourself. You don't weigh much more than Jamie.''

It wasn't strictly true, but she *didn't* weigh a whole lot. Funny, he'd always thought of Hannah as being the sturdy, homemaker type, but he rather liked the sensation of holding her slim body, soft and yielding against his harder angles. And though he'd initially regretted his proposal, a conviction of rightness came over him.

Yup, this was the best thing he could do. Hannah Liggett didn't have a chance. Even if she managed to say no to him, he didn't think anyone could say no to Jamie.

Hannah put her head against Ross's shoulder, resigned—if not happy—about being carried back to town like a silent-movie heroine.

What would everyone think?

Actually, she'd bet Ross was right. Depending on how they handled things, everyone in Quicksilver would think they'd always had a secret passion for one another. And Ten Penny *had* thought he was checking her out…not that Hannah believed Ross had actually been ogling her body. It could work.

Pooh.

Here she was, falling into line the way Ross expected. For years she'd stood up to brothers who towered over her, telling them when to get home and what chores to do. She'd kept her father's books and refused to let him pad charitable deductions on his tax returns. She'd even stared down a bear, intent on tasting her fresh-baked blueberry pie. But Ross McCoy had turned her into a quivering, compliant simpleton in two short hours.

Hannah moaned and buried her face deeper into his shirt. She had to be out of her mind to consider marrying the man. A sane woman would start running and never look back.

"Hannah?" Ross sounded alarmed and he stopped dead in his tracks. "What's wrong? Is something else hurting?"

"Nothing you can fix."

Well, he could fix *some* of it, but he wasn't interested. Her sexual appeal obviously rated about zero in his book.

Ross shrugged the shoulder beneath her cheek, encouraging her to look up. "Talk to me. I can't do anything if I don't know what's wrong."

Hannah glanced up at his worried frown and sighed. Even as a boy, he'd had an overdeveloped sense of responsibility—so serious and intense. He didn't understand why she was upset, but he wanted to fix it anyway.

"Hannah?"

"If you keep standing in the middle of the street, you'll get run over," she said practically, avoiding the real question altogether. After all, he couldn't help it if she wasn't sexy.

Ross scanned the so-called street and lifted one eyebrow. "Run down by what? A moose?"

"It could happen."

"Not in a million years." Nevertheless, he started walking again, covering the distance to the restaurant in less than a minute—downtown Quicksilver measured just over a hundred feet long.

"What's wrong?" Edgar Liggett exclaimed, throwing open the door for them.

"Nothing, Dad."

"Hannah turned her ankle and I felt like carrying her," Ross said calmly. He looked down at Hannah and smiled, enjoying the defiant sparkle in her eyes. "She's such a cozy armful, you can't blame me for taking advantage."

"Hot damn, didn't I tell you?" cackled Ten Penny. "I could tell by the way he was gawkin' at her. That boy's got one thing on his mind, and it ain't drinkin' no cup of coffee."

"See?" Ross whispered. "They aren't laughing. They think I'm hot for you."

"Which we both know isn't true," she hissed back, squirming in an attempt to gain her freedom. "Let me down."

Instead, Ross sat down himself, holding her securely on his lap. Her squirming continued until he pinched her bottom and muttered a "Stop that" command in her ear. As for being hot for Hannah—all that feminine wriggling was having a predictable effect on his body. He needed her to stay put and hide the evidence from everyone else...though it was like using gunpowder to put out a fire.

"You get everything straight with my girl?" asked Edgar Liggett, his expression turning rather fierce.

Hmmm.

Hannah might claim her father wasn't protective, but Ross didn't appreciate the way Edgar was examining him. He guessed it was one thing for a father to talk about his daughter getting married, and quite another to face the man who might be taking that married daughter to bed.

"Oh, we're pretty straight about everything, Mr. Liggett. Isn't that right, sweetheart?"

The look Hannah shot him wasn't exactly friendly. "I'm still thinking about it, darling. Remember?"

Her *darling* didn't sound nearly as affectionate as his "sweetheart," so he leaned forward. "Work with me on this, okay?" he murmured. "You're blowing the 'in love since we were kids' act. Trust me."

"You're enjoying this too much to be trusted." Hannah's whisper sounded more like a growl and he couldn't help chuckling.

Well, hell. He *was* having fun. Maybe he should have taken Hannah's temper into account before proposing, but the die was cast and he didn't really care. A woman needed some sass to get by in Alaska. "I'm just trying to be convincing."

"Ha."

She squirmed some more and Ross winced as her bottom pressed against the most vulnerable part of his anatomy.

"You planning on a long engagement?" called one of the ladies in the corner.

"Not very long." Ross answered before Hannah could say something different. He looked around and saw his son curled up asleep on a chair—at the moment Jamie looked a lot more peaceful than his father. "We're thinking about flying down to Nevada," he said with sudden inspiration. "You can get married in a hour in Reno. There's no waiting period."

Hannah gasped and dug an elbow into his ribs.

No pain, no gain.

"We're going tomorrow," he continued, gritting his teeth. "I don't want to give Hannah a chance to change her mind. Isn't that right, Honeycomb?"

"You, you..." she stuttered, plainly searching for something potent enough to fling at him.

He'd gone too far and he knew it, but he was truly a desperate man. Releasing his hold on Hannah's hip, Ross cupped the back of her head and pulled her into a kiss. Whatever expletive she'd been planning got smothered by his mouth.

"If that don't beat all," Ten Penny crowed. "I always knowed that boy had a fire in his belly. It's them quiet ones you gotta watch out for."

"Mmmrmph" was all Hannah could manage through the assault on her lips. She should have said something suitably scathing, but her thoughts were getting mushy. But it wasn't her fault; this was practically her first kiss, and none of the others had been so...intimate.

Ross's expertise was obvious; even in her muddled state she recognized it. His lips moved with supple, mobile strength across her mouth, coaxing and asking for something she didn't understand. The depth of her own inexperience cut unhappily through her mind and she froze.

Did Ross know? Did he realize how little she knew about men? Life in Quicksilver might have been sheltered from a romantic standpoint, but Hannah knew a lot of men wanted a woman with a certain level of experience.

Ross shifted, pulling her into full contact with his body, and she sucked in a breath. Her breasts ached and her nipples tightened like they did when she jumped into the shower and the water was too cold.

So, that's what it feels like, Hannah thought in wonderment...and some annoyance. Ross was playing dirty, and he shouldn't be allowed to get away with such a sneaky tactic. If she decided to marry him, it wouldn't be because of some fake seduction scene, staged for everyone's benefit. Threading her fingers through his hair, Hannah pulled. *Hard.*

His kiss turned into a growl, but he released her.

Hannah took advantage of the moment and scooted from Ross's lap. She wondered at the pained expression in his face, but only for a second.

"Did you get enough to eat?" she asked brightly…and to no one in particular. The small discomfort from her ankle erased any lingering mental fog. It served her right for not watching where she stepped.

"Mighty tasty chili," said Joe, who belched and patted his stomach. "Me an' the missus better be headin' home, though. Gotta break in that new mattress."

"Oh, Joe."

His bride let out a playful giggle and flipped the end of her feather boa at him. For an instant the years peeled away and Hannah glimpsed the audacious woman she must have been, braving the Alaska frontier with nothing but her personal attributes to support her. It wasn't the choice Hannah would have made, but Ten Penny was a law unto herself.

Though they'd been temporarily distracted, everyone began grinning and nudging one another. A marriage proposal was one thing, but they had a real live chivaree to attend. After more than seventy years of staying single in a territory where men outnumbered women, nobody was going to cheat Ten Penny out of a traditional wedding night.

In short order the occupants of the restaurant found the door and disappeared. The only ones left were Ross, her father and Jamie, who was beginning to wake up.

"Well," said her father, slapping his hands together. "It's all worked out nicely, hasn't it, Hannah?"

She smiled...showing a lot of teeth. "You knew about this, didn't you, Dad?"

The two men exchanged glances and her eyes narrowed.

"Ross called a few days ago and asked if you were seeing anyone else," Edgar admitted. "He mentioned he might fly over here for a visit. And I must say, I always thought he had a special fondness for you."

Amazing. Hannah could see her father almost believed his convenient fantasy. "You did, huh?"

"Yes, I—"

"Papa?" Jamie said, sitting up and rubbing his eyes. "My tummy hurts."

"I'm here, tiger." Ross sat next to the boy and patted his back. His expression told her everything—fierce, protective and totally lost. He didn't have a clue what to do next. "Hannah, what's wrong? Should we call the doctor?"

Oh, dear.

How could she resist a man like that? Strong and capable...yet totally inexperienced when it came to children. Without even trying, he was enticing her into his marriage scheme. She sighed and squared her shoulders. "Kids get a lot of tummy aches, Ross. Especially after a party."

"Yeah, but—"

"Don't worry, you're overreacting," Hannah said, limping across the room and kneeling next to Jamie. "Hey, kiddo. I'm sorry you don't feel so good. Do you want to come back to my house for a while?"

Jamie nodded and crawled down from the chair and

into her arms. His compact body snuggled close…and right into her heart, she feared. She stroked the hair back from his forehead. It was warm, but nothing to worry about; boys being boys, she suspected he'd charmed his way into a lot more cake and ice cream than he should have eaten.

"Okay, let's go. It's not far. We can walk."

"What about your ankle?" Ross murmured.

Honestly. Her ankle was barely sprained. Walking wouldn't hurt it any, but she was tired of arguing with the man.

"Dad?" Hannah called over her shoulder. "We need to borrow the truck. I think Ross and Jamie will have to spend the night with us. They can sleep in Deke's old bedroom."

A loud harumph came from behind them. "I don't think that's such a fine idea," said her father.

"Why?" she asked dryly. "You thought it was a fine idea to arrange a marriage behind my back. What difference can it make if Ross sleeps at the house?"

"That's different."

"It always is. To think I told Ross you weren't the protective sort."

"Why…how could you think that?" Edgar said, obviously shocked. "You're my little girl. And I didn't arrange any marriage," he asserted as he handed the keys to Ross. "Nobody does that any more."

Hannah rolled her eyes.

"Except in Alaska," she muttered. Yet she was touched that he'd worry about her virtue. Until now there hadn't been much cause for him to worry, so no wonder it was a surprise to find he had the same huffy puffy bluster of every other father on the planet.

"I'll put Jamie in the truck, then come back for you," Ross murmured, lifting his son.

"Huh." She made a face at his back. "You don't need to pretend any more, your audience is gone. I'm capable of walking under my own steam."

Turning at the door, he winked. "Just staying in practice, darling."

She rubbed the back of her neck and shook her head. Jamie must have gotten his charm from his father, because that man could charm a wolverine from its den.

"Dad, are you keeping the bar open tonight?" Hannah asked, trying to keep her voice from shaking. All at once it was too much—the wedding reception, Ross's appearance...his marriage proposal. A woman liked to think about these things; only, Ross didn't seem willing to wait a single day.

Reno.

She made another face, though it made the most sense; Ross wanted to get married before his ex-wife could file for custody again. Hannah didn't know a lot about custody battles, but she could see it might look better to a judge. And it would be a lot easier getting married in Reno, than doing it in Quicksilver and trying to pretend they were in love. *If* they got married, that is. She still wasn't sure it was such a good idea.

"Dad, the bar," Hannah repeated.

"They'll be wanting a sip or two after the chivaree," Edgar murmured. "Best to keep it open."

"I should stay and clean up."

"Go on, Hannah. You've done enough here." Her father angrily swiped the ancient bar with a rag, and he seemed to be talking about more than the restaurant.

"You spent eighteen years taking care of your brothers."

"Dad…"

"It was wrong to keep you, but your mama was gone, leaving me with a new baby and more to raise. I know it all fell on your shoulders."

"I didn't mind."

"I minded…more now than ever. You had a right to your life, and it's time you got something for yourself. Ross McCoy would make you a good husband."

"We don't love each other," Hannah said quietly.

"Love can come after. And if it doesn't…well, you were always good friends." Edgar put his hands down and stared at them. "Hannah, he's a fine man. He'd never hurt you."

She nodded thoughtfully. Ross *wouldn't* do anything to hurt her, at least not deliberately. And their friendship was nothing to sneeze at; despite a three-year age difference, they'd spent a lot of time together.

The bell over the door jangled and Edgar straightened, once more scrubbing the bar with furious intent.

"Ready?" asked Ross.

She stood, silently daring her "fiancée" to pick her up again. "I'll see you later, Dad."

"Think about what I said."

Hannah drew a shaky breath. "I'll be sure to do that."

The night wind rustled through the trees surrounding the house, the whispering sound as familiar to Hannah as the dancing northern lights in the midnight sky.

She turned in the bed, listening to the voices of nature and her own heart, trying to make a decision.

Over and over she replayed the day's events through her head, torn by emotions she hadn't felt for a long while.

Did a woman ever *really* give up dreams of white lace and forever-after love? Ten Penny hadn't. After all was said and done, Ten Penny had married for love. True, she'd spent ninety odd years finding that love and worked in a bawdy house in the meantime, but she'd married for the right reason.

"Blast," Hannah mumbled, kicking the blankets aside. She looked at herself in the old, yellowed mirror and grimaced. Her hair was neither blond nor brown, and she was reasonably well endowed, but that was all. Nothing spectacular. Just the basics. She certainly didn't inspire any overwhelming romantic urges in the opposite sex.

It had been years since she'd indulged in romantic daydreams; the local men weren't the type to inspire fantasies. And even if she'd felt something for one of them, they'd never looked at her twice, not with the commitment she felt to her family. By now, the ones her age were either married or had moved away.

Hannah wandered into the kitchen and set a pot of milk on the stove—might as well make hot chocolate and enjoy being sleepless.

"Make extra for me," said a quiet voice from the shadows.

Ross.

He stepped from the screened porch surrounding the rear of the house and leaned on the doorjamb. His unsnapped jeans rode low on his hips, and the rest of him was magnificently bare—feet, arms, shoulders. Hannah swallowed and looked back at the stove.

Don't think about it.

Right.

Good advice.

Now she just had to follow that advice, and she'd be fine. If she married Ross, she'd have to remember exactly *why* she was doing it: to become Jamie's mother. Nothing more. And since Jamie was such a darling little thing, that wouldn't be so hard, would it?

"Couldn't sleep, either?" he asked.

"It was a busy day. How is Jamie doing?"

Ross's shoulders lifted and fell, and a look of chagrin crossed his face. "You were right. He's fine—sound asleep, all curled up in the middle of the bed."

"Taking his half out of the middle?"

"Something like that."

"You get used to that with kids and cats. They have their own way of doing things." Hannah stirred the ingredients into the steaming pot, then poured the chocolate into two cups. She handed one to Ross and backed away quickly.

"Hey, I'm not going to bite," he murmured.

"That's reassuring."

A low chuckle rumbled from his chest, then his smile faded. "Is it so terrible, asking you to be Jamie's mother? He's a terrific kid."

Hannah traced the smooth edge of her cup, then shook her head. "I know you're just trying to do the best for him. If he was mine, I'd do the same thing. I'm flattered you think marrying me is 'doing the best' for him."

Sighing, Ross put his cup on the table and sat next to Hannah. He'd messed up badly, but there wasn't any going backward; he might as well round out the day with another unfair maneuver.

"Say, do you remember the last time we had hot chocolate together?"

She didn't look up, but he detected a small smile curving her lips. "In the clearing. You built a fire and made the worst cocoa I've ever drunk—from water, malted milk balls and a chocolate bar."

"At the time you said it was wonderful."

"I lied."

Ross laughed; he couldn't help himself. How could he have forgotten the way Hannah made him laugh? She'd always loved pulling his leg. Even at the worst of times she'd managed to drag a laugh from him with her teasing.

She looked at him from under her lashes with another slow smile. "Actually, I was right the first time—it *was* wonderful. You were so sweet to me that day, anything would have tasted good. I think our best and worst moments together have happened in that clearing."

Whoa.

Ross felt his blood go up a few degrees from the smile—and from the worn, oversize T-shirt she wore for sleeping. The soft cotton molded her breasts with loving faithfulness, something she didn't seem to realize. Nor did she seem to realize there were worn places in the fabric that made it nearly transparent.

Don't stare, Ross reminded himself.

A gentleman should keep his eyes directed elsewhere. But more importantly, he didn't want to find Hannah attractive, not in that way. When it got right down to brass tacks, he didn't trust his judgment when love and sex were involved.

A marriage based on friendship was a much safer bet than the alternative. Hannah might not be his type romantically, but she was definitely a friend. They could be good together, just like when they were kids.

"So..." he said slowly. "How about marrying me? Have you made up your mind yet?"

Chapter Three

Hannah held her breath, arguments both for and against saying "yes" racing through her mind.

"Yes" to the wonderful possibilities of becoming a mother.

"No" to marrying a man she didn't love.

If she held out for love, she could end up like Ten Penny, spending most of her life without a family. Maybe *all* her life. But it didn't have to be like that; Ross was offering her a chance to become a mother, even if he hadn't done it in a tactful way.

She focused on Ross's intent face, hoping to find an answer.

Things had changed since they were children. Marriage to Ross McCoy meant leaving her home for good. It meant making all new friends and starting a completely different life. Talk about a girl from the sticks—she'd never been more than fifty miles from home.

None of it would matter if he was in love with her,

but she didn't have that luxury. And it hurt to admit, but Ross was right about something else: this *was* her chance to leave Quicksilver.

Maybe her last chance.

Hannah set her cup on the table. Okay, so they weren't in love. Big deal. If she married Ross, she'd be Jamie's mother, and eighteen years of on-the-job training *did* give her an edge in the maternal skills department.

"About this afternoon...what I said about giving you a good life? I wasn't implying you were mercenary," Ross said, as if searching for the right words. "But you're honestly entitled to wonder what this arrangement would mean to you."

Actually, Hannah thought it was all very simple. She'd get to be Jamie's mother, and Ross would get a wife to show the judge in case of a custody battle.

"I'm not wealthy, but I can afford to hire housekeepers and nannies and do anything necessary to take care of my son," Ross continued, a serious expression growing on his face. "So don't think I just want an inexpensive baby-sitter. I proposed because I want my son to have a mother who is sweet and loving and decent. And I swear I'd be a good husband and do everything possible to make you happy."

"As Jamie's mother," she added, wondering why it made her so sad. One by one her dreams had vanished over the years, and now Ross was offering one of the most precious of those dreams back to her. Why was she hesitating?

Ross lifted her hand and squeezed it, his fingers hard against her softer skin. "Jamie is part of this, but I want you to be happy because you're my friend. We can be partners."

Friends.

Partners.

Not husband and wife in a real sense. Not a marriage, but an "arrangement." Ross would keep her clothed and sheltered, and she'd be his son's mother. Hannah swallowed, knowing she had to ask if he expected anything else, even if it embarrassed them both.

"There's one thing we haven't talked about," she said slowly. "That is, we haven't discussed what our...uh, our personal relationship would be."

"I don't know what...*oh*." To Hannah's surprise, a dull red color crept into his face. "You're asking if I expect...er, want *all* the marital comforts."

A smile tugged at the corner of her mouth, though the situation wasn't funny. "That's one way of putting it."

Ross shifted uncomfortably. "To be honest, I hadn't thought that far ahead. I guess I assumed we'd have to get reacquainted, then make some sort of decision down the road."

"I see." It was a nice, noncommittal response that didn't mean anything, and Hannah kept her face neutral. She must not have been successful at hiding her feelings, because Ross leaned forward with a worried frown.

"It has nothing to do with you, Hannah. I just haven't considered that aspect of things. Hell, I was blinded by lust in my first marriage and it was a disaster. We didn't even last six months."

"I see," she repeated, understanding all too well. She was the perfect wife because he didn't find her desirable.

Well, fine. She wouldn't find him desirable, either.

"Hannah?"

The concerned look in his dark eyes made her sigh; if Ross was undesirable, then she was deaf and blind. But she'd have to try. They couldn't make a marriage work if they wanted different things from one another.

"Yes," she said abruptly.

He blinked. "Yes?"

"Yes, I'll marry you. For Jamie's sake," she added. And it *was* for Jamie's sake. Neither of them would be considering marriage under different circumstances—at least not to each other.

"Thank God," Ross said. He leaned forward and planted a kiss on her cheek. As an engagement kiss, it wasn't the most inspiring moment of Hannah's life. "What do think about getting married in Reno?" he asked. "It's fast and easy. We could get the whole thing over with tomorrow."

Her heart twinged when she thought about the alternative—the little church in Quicksilver. Her parents had wed there, along with all the people she knew; it wasn't fancy or glamorous, but it was home. In all the times she'd imagined getting married, a quickie wedding chapel in Reno had never entered her mind. But it was logical and sensible and the best thing to do, so Hannah drew a deep breath and plastered a smile on her face.

"That sounds great. I've never been to Nevada."

Ross chuckled. "Then it's going to be an experience—slot machines, bright lights, people rushing everywhere, plenty of excitement. I don't want Jamie getting too tired, so we'd better plan on spending the night."

"Okay." Hannah shivered, but not from cold. Everything seemed to be moving so fast. She'd never flown before, or left Alaska, or gotten married, and now it would all happen in single day. It was a little intimidating.

"We should leave early in the morning. We'll take my plane to Anchorage, then catch a flight to Reno from there."

She traced the rim of her cup with the tip of her finger. "I'll have to pack some things. Are you planning to come back to Quicksilver, or to your house in Kachelak?"

"Unless it's a problem, I thought we'd head for Kachelak," Ross said, watching Hannah closely. He didn't want to push; it was enough that she'd agreed to marry him. "Jamie needs a steady routine, so I want to get him home again. We'll work out how to get your things moved."

"Fine."

Ross breathed a sigh of relief. It was settled. The worst part was over; he'd proposed, Hannah had accepted and lightning hadn't struck.

With his luck in women, that was quite an accomplishment.

It wasn't that he had anything against women in general. He just couldn't confuse things with love and sex, particularly where his son was concerned.

Hannah rinsed her cup in the sink, then hesitated. "Well, good night."

"Good night." Just then a faint cranky sound from Jamie's bedroom caught his attention and Ross automatically climbed to his feet.

"I'll take care of him," she said. "Finish your cocoa."

"No, I'll do it. He's my son."

To his surprise, Hannah turned around, walked to him and poked her finger in his chest.

"Let's get one thing straight, Ross McCoy," she said sharply. "There won't be any 'my' in this arrangement. Jamie will be *our* son. That's the agreement. You can stuff your promises to take care of me and make me happy. I'm doing this because I want to be Jamie's mother. Period."

"I didn't mean it that way."

"Good. Don't forget it."

She turned again and walked out, her slender body still shaking with emotion.

"Phew!" Ross whistled beneath his breath, stunned by the sparks he'd seen in Hannah's eyes. He'd seen her upset before, but nothing like that...a she-cat fighting for her baby.

Yet a smile grew at the corners of his mouth and he settled back into his chair. He'd been unintentionally possessive, but he wanted a real mother for Jamie, and that's exactly what Jamie was getting. Hannah wouldn't back down or do anything she didn't think was right for *their* son.

He'd just have to make sure she never regretted marrying him. It might be a more practical arrangement than his first marriage, but it would be a lot more comfortable.

"Right." Ross nodded to himself and got up from the table. He needed to call the airline and make reservations for their flight to Reno.

Things were working out better than he had any right to expect.

Dawn was just a promise on the horizon when Hannah crept up to the attic and stood in the tiny space, debating whether she should look in her mother's belongings.

Of course, she knew what was there, and it all belonged to her—her father had been very clear on that
point. Yet she hadn't looked in those boxes since she'd
packed them, nearly eighteen years ago.

"Meroow?"

Doggit, her fourteen-pound calico cat, brushed
against her legs, a warm presence in the chilly room.
Hannah barely noticed the cold, too accustomed to
Alaska's climate to worry about a normal fall morning.
She did remember her mother had hated the cold,
nearly as much as she'd loved her husband. Mary Liggett had been born in South Carolina, which didn't
have the temperature extremes of Alaska.

A faint smile curved Hannah's mouth. South Carolina always sounded exotic and mysterious when her
mother talked about her childhood, painting images of
a place scented with magnolia blossoms, warm breezes
and Southern gentlemen who bowed and kissed a
lady's hand.

"Nobody kisses hands anymore," Hannah told
Doggit. "They probably didn't even when Mom lived
there."

Doggit licked her ankle and meowed again.

"Okay, I was partly wrong—some gentlemen kiss
your feet," she said, leaning down and stroking the
feline's neck. A rumbling purr came from Doggit's
furred chest. He'd earned his name from dogging her
heels as a kitten, never being more than a step behind
her.

Hannah looked again at the stack of boxes and
ached at the memories they raised…memories of being fourteen years old and packing her mother's things
away. Of tears falling so hard, she barely saw what
she was packing.

A murmur of voices drifted up through the floor-boards as Hannah knelt by the closest box. Her fingers brushed the dusty surface, still hesitating.

"Hannah, where are you?"

Ross. Hannah snatched her hand back with guilty speed, then laughed self-consciously. She had every right to go through her mother's belongings.

"Up here."

Ross appeared at the top of the staircase, his broad shoulders and powerful build even more overwhelming under the sloped roof.

It was just as well he didn't have any thought of making love to her, Hannah thought idly. Getting into bed with a man that tall could be rather intimidating. The thought sent a surge of heat to her cheeks and she ducked her head, hoping the low light would hide any telltale color.

"What's all of this?" he asked and gestured to the boxes.

"This?" Hannah swallowed. "My mother's dresses and books...and some other stuff. Dad always said they were mine."

"I understand." Ross put his hands in his pockets and smiled kindly. "Don't worry about getting everything to Kachelak. I called and talked to Mike Fitzpatrick. He's one of my partners, and he'll fly over today with his wife, Callie, to get a load of your things. He said it was a wedding present, since they can't come to the wedding."

"Oh. That's nice of them." Hannah bit the inside of her cheek and wished Ross would go away so she could finish her task in peace. The truth was, she didn't have anything special to wear during the ceremony, so she wanted to check her mother's wedding dress and see if it might be all right.

"And you don't need to worry about anything getting broken," Ross assured her. "Callie is terrific. She'll handle everything with kid gloves, and will make sure Mike does, too."

Callie is terrific.

Oh, great. That's all she needed, to hear her husband-to-be praise another woman on her wedding day.

"Hey, breakfast is ready," called her father.

Hannah sniffed the air and decided breakfast was *more* than ready. Her father had a distinct talent for destroying food and setting off smoke alarms. He usually left the restaurant kitchen alone, but home was another matter.

The restaurant.

Quicksilver's *only* restaurant. Hannah thought about it for a minute, then decided it would be okay. She mostly served coffee, and anyone could make coffee, including the customers. They probably wouldn't even miss her.

"Coming?"

Ross held out his hand and Hannah sighed, knowing she wouldn't be opening her mother's boxes anytime soon. It didn't really matter; after so many years, the dress would need washing and ironing, and probably wouldn't fit that well. Besides, Reno didn't seem a proper setting for her mother's antique wedding gown.

She climbed to her feet with Ross's assistance and brushed dust and cobwebs from her jeans. Under the eaves of the attic she saw a pair of almond-shaped eyes glinting, and she frowned. "I forgot. What about Doggit?" she asked.

"Who's Doggit?"

"Mrrow." Doggit nudged his head between her ankles and looked up at Ross.

"Ross McCoy, meet Doggit. He must have been shy last night, because you and Jamie were here. He's my cat," she announced with a trace of defiance. "I want him to live with us in Kachelak. But he doesn't go outside—he's sort of a wuss," she added.

Ross looked down at the whiskered face and grinned. Doggit was probably the ugliest cat in Alaska—maybe the ugliest on the planet—but he knew better than to insult Hannah's baby.

"It's my policy to always welcome in-laws," he said. "And you'd be a wuss, too, if you were that small and had bears for neighbors."

The feline blinked back at him with an undeniable charm.

"We'll call Callie and Mike and ask them to bring an animal carrier," Ross said. "Callie loves cats, so they'll get along just fine."

"All right," Hannah murmured, a dubious expression on her face. "But he's never flown before."

"They can bring tranquilizers, too, in case he needs them."

"Hmm." Hannah preceded him down the narrow steps and Ross paused to admire the gentle swing of her hips. Her jeans were worn to baby softness and they clung tightly to her curves.

When he looked up, Edgar Liggett was standing at the bottom of the stairs, holding a crackling iron fry pan. Smoke wreathed his frowning face and Ross shrugged uncomfortably.

Okay, so he'd been looking at Hannah's rear end. It was just aesthetic appreciation; a man could enjoy looking without planning to do something about it.

And anyway, they were getting married, so it wasn't Edgar's worry. Still, Ross had an urge to loosen his nonexistent collar. Fathers being fathers, he didn't think Edgar would agree with his reasoning.

It was lucky he'd straightened this out with Hannah; he wouldn't want her thinking he planned to jump her bones at the first opportunity. He couldn't believe he hadn't thought about it ahead of time. No wonder she was angry and insulted when he talked about providing for her—she must have wondered if he expected her to put out in return.

In the kitchen they found Hannah salvaging what she could of the meal. Edgar clunked the iron skillet back down on the stove. It contained a number of carbonized black lumps, unrecognizable from their original form.

"Er...sorry, Hannah," Edgar muttered. He scratched his head and stared at the pan. "I don't know how that happens."

"It's all right, Dad."

"I wanted to help out, you getting married today and all."

She guided him into a chair at the table and patted his shoulder. "I appreciate the thought."

It was a scene they'd obviously played a thousand times—her father apologizing and Hannah making him feel better for trashing her cookware.

Ross lifted Jamie from where he sat, yawning widely, and settled him on his lap. At least Hannah wouldn't have to worry about her husband setting fire to the house. He didn't aspire to gourmet cooking, but he knew how to fry an egg and boil water without burning it, though lately they'd been living on takeout pizza and hamburgers.

He tried to catch Hannah's attention as she started a pan of fried potatoes and ham, but she seemed distracted and he hoped she wasn't worried about her father managing alone.

Well, that was something he could help fix.

Ross cleared his throat. "Edgar, have you ever used a microwave?"

"Nope. Seen one once, up at Skagway."

"They're really handy and easy to work." Ross thought quickly, deciding the older man would need something foolproof; maybe a microwave with a single dial. And a large chest freezer to hold convenience foods. He could fly the stuff to Quicksilver once a month, and that way Hannah could visit on a regular basis. Jamie, too, since she'd want him to get acquainted with his new grandfather.

Grandfather. A warm sensation crept around Ross's heart. In the years since his divorce he'd thought of marriage as the ultimate trap, something to avoid at all cost. Yet by marrying Hannah, he was getting a family again, not only for Jamie, but for himself. With his own parents gone, it was an unexpected gift.

Hannah carried cups to the table and filled them with steaming coffee. "What are you plotting?" she murmured, setting one by his elbow.

"How to feed your dad without risking a house-size bonfire," he whispered back.

Her eyes widened and she shot a quick glance at her father. "That isn't your—"

"Responsibility?" Ross finished. "I meant what I said about being partners. After all, he's not just *your* father, he's *our* father." He grinned and winked. "If you're worried about him, then so am I."

"Worried about who?" Edgar asked, apparently hearing something of their conversation.

"Nobody, Dad."

He snorted and took a long drag of hot coffee.

"We just wondered if you wanted to fly to Reno with us," Ross said with a sudden flash of inspiration. "You're welcome to come."

For a moment Edgar brightened, then he shook his head. "Naw, I got things I have to do here," he muttered.

"But I'm sure Hannah would really like—"

"This is a busy time at the bar," Hannah interrupted, sending him a warning glance. "Dad can't get away."

Too late, Ross remembered Edgar had a fear of flying. He'd fought in Vietnam and been shot down twice, barely surviving the second crash. The military had finally sent him home on a ship, because he hadn't been able to face another plane.

Now his daughter was marrying a pilot, and the old guy had been a real trouper about the whole thing. Ross wouldn't have blamed him for saying "No, don't ever look at Hannah again." Instead, Edgar had been thrilled.

Well...thrilled about the proposal.

He still wasn't enthusiastic about the *looking*, Ross reflected. It must be hard for a man to see his daughter grow up and get married.

"I understand," he said. "It's hard getting away from my business, too, and I've got two partners to fill in for me."

His comment earned him a warm smile from Hannah, who urged her father to wash up in the bathroom.

"Thanks," she murmured when they were alone. "He can't help it."

"I should have thought before saying anything." But a new thought occurred to Ross and he looked up. "By the way, have *you* ever flown before?"

"No." She shook her head, looking uncomfortable.

Ross shifted in his chair and whistled beneath his breath. This was interesting. If she had the same fear as her father, he might be getting married in Alaska after all. It wouldn't be as convenient timewise, but he had no intention of forcing Hannah onto a plane if she wasn't willing to go.

"Uh…are you sure you're okay about flying to Nevada?"

She smiled brightly and nodded. "Of course. I can't wait to see a real-live slot machine. It's going to be fun."

Fun.

Ross took a large swallow of coffee. In his experience, marriage wasn't the least bit fun, but with Hannah in the picture, you could never tell.

Chapter Four

"This is awful," Hannah muttered to herself.

She scowled and looked at the clothes in her closet for the tenth time. No matter how hard she tried, nothing could turn those few garments into a wedding dress. There was a dark blue shirtwaist she'd worn to a funeral, a dress three sizes too big that her father had gotten her in Skagway, and assorted shirts and jeans.

The best she could manage was clean and neat and not too old. Not that Ross would care. He'd probably be uncomfortable at the thought of dressing up for the wedding—that would make it too much of an event. A marriage of convenience wasn't an event, it was a business arrangement. The fact they were friends didn't change anything.

"How long do you need, Hannah?" called Ross from the hallway.

She wrinkled her nose at the question. Considering

her wardrobe, she could be packed in ten minutes and still have time for a cup of coffee. "Not long."

"We should leave as soon as possible, in case there's a delay in Anchorage."

"Okay. Go ahead and get Jamie into the truck. I'll be out in a few minutes." Hannah began stuffing her clothing into an old suitcase. It wasn't as if she didn't have everything she needed. What could anyone need in Quicksilver? The basics were more than enough.

Unsure how quickly they'd get married once they reached Reno, Hannah put on her newest pair of jeans and one of her white shirts. She looked in the mirror and shrugged philosophically. She'd look silly in a fancy wedding dress, and this way she was comfortable. Most of her favorite jeans and tops were really old, since she preferred the softness of well-washed fabric on her skin.

Doggit lay on the bed, an unhappy look on his face. Cats were creatures of habit, and he never wanted anything to change. "It's all right," she whispered as she rubbed his ear. "I'll see you soon."

"Mrroww." His claws caught her sleeve as she pulled her hand away. Dear Doggit, she was the only person he truly cared about, and now his world was turning upside down.

"I have to go, baby." Hannah unhooked his claws and gave him a last stroke. "I'll see you in Kachelak."

She checked to see he had plenty of food and water, then closed the bedroom door and taped a note to Ross's "terrific" Callie on the knob. It explained about Doggit's favorite hiding places—a stranger would have a hard time catching the timid feline.

"I'll take that," said Ross when Hannah walked into the kitchen, suitcase in hand.

A little surprised, she gave the case to Ross and followed him to the truck where Jamie and her father waited. Her brothers were okay, but it wouldn't occur to them to carry her suitcase. Buried deep in the Liggett male subconscious was the notion that sisters weren't actually women…they were people-shaped machines who cooked food, took care of the laundry and sewed on missing buttons.

Ross set the suitcase in the bed of the old truck and put his hand on her elbow as she climbed into the cab. Hannah shot him another surprised look.

"Uh…thanks," she said.

A faint frown appeared on his forehead. "No problem. It'll be a tight fit in there with four of us, but I can hold Jamie."

"No, I'll take him."

Jamie gave her a shy smile and readily climbed into her lap for the short trip to the airstrip. Hannah cuddled him close, trying not to notice the feel of Ross's body next to her. Tight fit was right. Sandwiched between the two tall men, she had little more than breathing space. It wasn't a new sensation—not after living with six large brothers—but with Ross it seemed different.

Great, she thought to herself. She was supposed to remember they were just friends and that she didn't want anything else. And I don't, Hannah assured herself stoutly.

Biting her lip, Hannah concentrated on the sight of the plane as they approached Quicksilver's "official" airstrip. While she'd never flown before, no one could grow up in Alaska without learning something about airplanes. It was a Piper Navajo, and she could see Ross kept it in top condition.

And it looked awfully small.

Of course, everybody said the Piper was a good plane, so she didn't have anything to worry about. A flutter of nerves went through her tummy and she looked down at Jamie again.

"Do you like to fly?" she asked.

Jamie thought about it for a long moment, then nodded his head decisively. "Papa goes high up and swoosh down." He imitated the plane's movement with his fingers and her stomach turned.

High.

Swoosh down?

Still, Hannah doubted Ross was a barnstorming type of pilot, particularly with his son on board. It probably just *seemed* dramatic to a young child.

"That's nice. I've never flown before, so I'd really appreciate some help."

"Okay."

Hannah hid a smile as Jamie straightened his shoulders with determination. His resemblance to his father was stronger than ever and she cast a sideways glance at Ross. He sat comfortably on the seat, his long legs stretched out as far as the space would allow and his arm resting on the open frame of the window. He didn't appear to be paying attention to the conversation, but she figured he didn't miss much when it came to his son.

Her father braked to a halt in front of the Piper and held his arms out to Jamie. "Come on, lad," he said. "Let's get ever'thing on the plane."

The two walked around to back of the pickup, gabbing comfortably away. They were already the best of friends—after six sons, Edgar had a knack with little boys.

Ross didn't open his own door and Hannah wondered if he was reconsidering his crazy plan. Marriage? Lord knew, she'd reconsidered it a couple thousand times herself. And once they took off, it would be ever harder to change their minds. Though...she'd probably be too petrified to think about anything except flying for the first time in her life.

"You don't have to worry, I'm a good pilot, Honeycomb," Ross murmured. "But we can do this another way if you want. I'd never do something you didn't want."

Her eyes narrowed. Drat the man. He might be a good pilot, but he read minds, too. She suspected it could be an annoying habit in a husband.

"I'm fine," she said.

"You're whiter than January snow," he retorted.

Hannah took a steadying breath and glared. "I'm entitled. Now let's get going. You *did* say we have a flight to catch in Anchorage. Didn't you?" She scooted past the steering wheel and out through the driver's door.

"Yeah." Ross whistled beneath his breath and got out himself. More and more he regretted his suggestion they get married in Reno. It seemed a fine idea at the time, but he'd miscalculated a few things...such as his bride-to-be's inexperience with planes.

On the other hand, Hannah was marrying a pilot. She'd have to fly sooner or later, and sooner was usually better with this kind of thing.

If Hannah's face was white, then Edgar's was green by the time they'd loaded their few pieces of luggage into the tail section and put Jamie in the back seat. He mumbled something about not waiting for them to take off, then stood fumbling with the truck keys.

"I'll see you soon, Dad," said Hannah, giving him a hug. "We'll come back to visit, and I'll call."

"You do that." Edgar shuffled his feet and blinked several times, having years of practice as a gruff old coot who didn't like showing his emotions. "And you phone after getting there. You're staying the night, right?"

Ross nodded. "It's too tiring for Jamie to go down and come back on a midnight flight."

"And Hannah, too," Edgar added. "You said you'd take good care of my girl."

"Dad!" Hannah shook her head and rolled her eyes in apparent disgust.

"Of course." Ross was embarrassed. He didn't mind Edgar being protective of Hannah, and he hadn't meant to exclude her from his comment. But it was strange thinking about someone else after being divorced and fighting to get custody of Jamie for so long. He needed practice in *sounding* like a good provider, as well as being one.

With another few muttered words, Edgar climbed in his truck and drove away, the vehicle bouncing on the rough, graveled road. When he'd disappeared, Hannah stopped waving and turned around with an annoyed expression.

"I realize you and my father are cut from the same cloth—primitive macho males who think they know better than the rest of the world—but I can take care of myself, thank you."

"We didn't mean anything by it."

"Sure."

Ross felt a grin pulling at the corners of his mouth, but he didn't think it was wise to smile at this point. Then he remembered her reaction when he'd carried her suitcase, and the desire to smile faded. He didn't want to fault Edgar, but it seemed as if Hannah had been taking care of everyone for so long, that everyone had forgotten to take care of *her*.

"Uh…let's discuss it later," he said. He didn't want to get into a debate about her family, and he certainly didn't want to argue over the way he planned to treat her. Hannah deserved a little pampering, whether she agreed or not.

"I want to discuss it now."

He reached out and tugged the thick braid of hair hanging over her left shoulder. It was the color of a mellowed brass kettle and glinted in the sunlight.

"You sure turned into an argumentative little thing. Do you know that?"

"We always argued…and I'm *not* little," she added.

It was just like the previous day when she'd said she was too heavy to carry, and Ross shook his head in amazement. Hannah had such an air of competence and energy, you didn't notice she was only five foot three, with slender bones and delicate features. The rest of her family was so tall, she probably looked even smaller standing in the middle of them.

"I guess we did argue," he drawled. "Nice to know things haven't changed."

At least they haven't changed that much, Ross added silently, except now they were adults and Hannah had turned into an attractive woman. Only, he didn't feel comfortable thinking that way, so he pushed the thought from his mind.

Hannah gave him one of her suspicious looks and he shrugged. The suspicion probably came from raising her brothers—six boys must have gotten into plenty of mischief. He was darned lucky she was willing to go through it again with Jamie.

"Shall we go?" he asked, looking at his watch.

"We haven't settled anything. You just changed the subject," Hannah retorted.

Ross reminded himself that obstinacy was a plus when you lived in Alaska. You needed a certain amount of pure cussedness to get through months of short days and freezing temperatures. And it could work in his favor if he handled things right.

"Hannah, are you trying to delay leaving? Like I said, if you're too nervous about flying, we can get married here in Alaska."

As he'd expected, her lips pressed together and she marched toward the Piper Navajo with a stiff back.

Ross sighed. If he thought Hannah was *that* afraid, he'd break his own arm before goading her onto the plane. As it was, he just didn't want to argue about something so silly.

Of *course* he planned to take care of her. Maybe it was old-fashioned, but he'd feel compelled to take care of any woman wearing his ring. It didn't matter that it was a marriage of convenience...too bad if she thought that was a primitive macho male attitude.

He hadn't thought so, but apparently he was a primitive, macho male kind of guy.

Hannah relaxed into the cushioned seat of the airliner and tried to ignore the faint queasiness in her stomach. Nerves. She'd come to the conclusion it had less to do with flying, and more to do with getting married.

Flying wasn't so bad once you got used to the idea there was nothing but air beneath you. She glanced out the window and watched the distant ground for a moment. It didn't look real...and it was an awfully long way away.

"How are you doing?" Ross asked for the thousandth time since they'd taken off.

"Fine."

The first-class flight attendant came by, offering them something to eat or drink, also for the thousandth time. The woman's gaze always remained fixed on Ross, even when she was talking to Jamie, and Hannah gritted her teeth. It was bad enough looking like a reject from a hickstown, but she'd obviously been dismissed as a friend or sister, not someone with a romantic role in his life.

Of course, she *didn't* have a romantic role, but the flight attendant had no way of knowing that.

"I don't know about my fiancé, but I'd like some..." Hannah searched in her mind for something appropriately sophisticated. Unfortunately, she wouldn't recognize *sophisticated* if it hit her in the face. "Uh, I'd like some tea."

At the word *fiancé,* the other woman turned red. "Of course. Would you like lemon with that?"

"Just tea, thank you."

Ross choked and covered his mouth with his hand. Hannah might object to him being a primitive macho male, but she wasn't above a little feminine shoulder bumping herself. My fiancé? Whether she realized it or not, she'd just put down territorial markers; as the "territory" in question, he thought it was a riot.

"Are *you* all right?" Hannah asked pointedly.

He cleared his throat. "No problem."

She twisted in her seat and Ross tried to keep from seeing the way her shirt gaped in the front. From his vantage point he could see the soft swells of her breasts confined by a simple cotton bra. There was nothing deliberately provocative about the way she was dressed, yet he was provoked nonetheless.

Don't think about it.

Good advice, but he was lousy on taking good advice these days.

McCoy, you're slime. You propose an honorable arrangement, and then you go ballistic over the woman's chest. Hannah's chest, he reminded his better self. His good buddy, who'd never turned him on before. Of course, she was also a kid then, but it was the idea that counted. Hands off.

"So watch it, McCoy," he muttered.

"What?" she asked.

"Nothing."

"Hmm."

Ross wondered what the "hmm" meant, but he wasn't going to ask. Nothing about their relationship was working out the way he'd expected. Somehow Hannah managed to be exactly the way he remembered, and still remained a complete mystery. Maybe she was always this way and he'd been blind all those years ago.

"Papa?" Jamie peered over the seat in front of them. The plane wasn't full, so the flight attendant had offered to let him stretch out on an empty pair of seats for a nap.

"Yes, Jamie?"

"Are we there yet?"

Ross checked his watch. "Another hour." He glanced at Hannah, then back at Jamie. They hadn't explained the purpose for their trip, and now would be as good a time as any. "Why don't you come around and sit on my lap so Hannah and I can talk to you?''

Jamie nodded and lunged over the seat, rather than walking around. He laughed when his foot got caught, requiring Hannah to hold him upside down while Ross extricated the trapped limb.

''Phew.'' Ross wanted to scold Jamie, but the flushed, happy look on his son's face made the words strangle in his throat. Somehow Jamie had ended on Hannah's lap instead of his own, but he didn't mind. It gave him a chance to watch them together. His doubts about getting married always faded when he saw Jamie with Hannah—they were so natural together.

''You have to be careful,'' she said, ''or the cushion monster will catch you.''

Jamie cocked his head and considered the matter with a skeptical expression. Clearly he wasn't too convinced about things like cushion monsters. ''The cushion monster?''

''Yup. It's soft and squishy and it does stuff like this.'' She tickled him lightly and he giggled.

Well, if Hannah didn't think Jamie needed scolding, Ross wasn't going to object. Perhaps she thought her new son needed fun and smiles more than he needed words of discipline.

''Jamie…?''

Jamie looked up. ''Yes, Papa?''

''We're going to Reno so Hannah and I can get married. Do you know what that means?''

''Dory says it's like going to the bank. Are you going to the bank, Papa?''

The words jolted through Ross. It was bad enough that Doreen had neglected Jamie, but she'd passed on her warped philosophy, as well. "Uh, that's not exactly what it means to get married. At least it's not supposed to be," he added grimly.

"Who's Dory?" Hannah asked.

"My ex-wife." He looked at her horrified expression and winced. He hadn't told her everything about his divorce, but his son's guileless comment probably explained things pretty well.

Hannah smoothed Jamie's hair and kissed the top of his head. "Getting married means you want to spend your life with someone special," she said softly. "And it means I get to be your mother and take care of you. Does that sound all right?"

Jamie thought about it for a solemn minute. "Can I call you Mommy?"

Hannah's heart felt like it was ready to burst, but she managed to nod. "I'd like that."

He reached up and patted her cheek. "Okay."

A surge of both pleasure and sorrow went through Hannah. Jamie was such a sweet child. He really needed a lot of brothers and sisters to teach him how to play, but considering Ross's plan for their marriage, brothers and sisters weren't likely. And it was too bad—Ross needed a big family almost as much as Jamie.

The pilot's voice came over the speaker system, saying they'd be landing in Reno shortly, and to fasten their seat belts. Hannah let Ross take Jamie as she snapped her belt. It wasn't takeoff that made her the most nervous, it was landing.

Takeoff was fun, with a rush of power that pressed you back in the seat—in a big plane, that is. In Ross's Piper, the plane seemed to levitate off the ground with hardly any effort.

They'd carried their small amount of luggage aboard with them, so they were able to leave the airport without waiting for baggage to be unloaded. Everything was dryer and hotter than in Alaska, the mid-afternoon sun putting out waves of stifling heat. Hannah opened another button on her shirt and fanned herself.

"Too warm?" Ross asked as he climbed in behind her in the taxicab.

She lifted her shoulders and dropped them. "I've never been anywhere but Quicksilver and Skagway. It doesn't get this hot back home."

"A lot of people enjoy the heat, but we'll check into the hotel first," Ross said. "We can cool off for a while, then have dinner and find a chapel once the temperature goes down. You can swim if you want—I made reservations at a place with several pools."

"Oh...won't it be too late to get married later?" Hannah's stomach began churning again and she gulped. "Everything will be closed."

He grinned wryly. "Nope. You can get married until midnight in this town. They say New York never sleeps, but it's got nothing on Reno. And since this is high desert country, it'll get cooler once the sun goes down."

She glanced at him and wondered how Ross knew so much about getting married in Nevada. If she found out he'd married his first wife in Reno, she'd probably hit him. "What about a license?"

"A license?" He looked at her blankly, which made her feel better. "I don't know. Maybe we get it at the chapel. Driver?" he said to the cabdriver. "Do you know anything about getting married?"

"Sure! Twenty-seven years I've been married. You

folks tying the knot?'' the other man asked. He gave Hannah a cheerful smile when she nodded and asked about the license. ''The license you need to get at the courthouse, but it's open very late. And my wife's second cousin, Joe, has a nice wedding chapel. You go there—it's good luck to get married at Joe's.''

Personally, Hannah didn't think anything was lucky about this marriage, but she wasn't in any position to judge. At the moment she was hot and breathless and going into sensory overload.

They were driving down a broad street, edged on either side with brilliantly lit casinos. Lights and billboards vied with hawkers carrying signs and shouting at the passing cars. Hundreds of people spilled out doorways and along the sidewalks, wearing brightly colored shorts and halter tops and printed T-shirts. It was the nosiest, most gaudy place she'd ever seen.

After a few minutes they stopped in front of a huge hotel casino on a small rise of land. Even to Hannah's inexperienced eye, it was a lavishly expensive resort.

The cabdriver appeared to have adopted them, because he insisted on taking their luggage inside and personally escorting them to the registration desk.

''These are my good friends, so we take good care of them,'' he said to the hotel staff. ''Yes?''

''Of course.'' The dark-suited gentleman behind the glossy black counter looked like he'd just bitten into a lemon. Obviously he didn't appreciate the informality of their driver. ''We take excellent care of all our guests.'' He deliberately turned his attention to Ross and Jamie, then Hannah, who gave him a tentative smile.

''Hello,'' she murmured.

A flicker of warmth rose in the man's eyes and he

smiled back. "Ma'am, we have a fine child-care service, so you'll be able to enjoy our casinos without worry."

"We won't be visiting the casinos," Ross informed him. "We're—"

"Hannah's going to be my new mommy," Jamie interrupted. He let go of Ross's shirt and clapped his hands in excitement. "Papa and Hannah are getting married."

Everyone looked at Hannah and she blushed.

Other employees moved closer, their attention caught by Jamie's high-pitched voice. An echo of "Congratulations" followed, turning her pink cheeks even brighter.

Ross handed Jamie to Hannah and watched his son and fiancée beguile the hotel staff. They had to be jaded, working in a place like Reno, but they seemed genuinely captivated by her shy innocence.

Mentally, he went over a list of things he needed to do before they could get married—on the very top was getting a ring for his blushing bride-to-be. But it shouldn't be a problem; there was a jewelry store in the lower level of the hotel, and they'd have something suitable.

Ross grinned and filled out the registration form someone absently pushed in his direction. Hannah was right. This trip to Reno was turning out to be a lot of fun.

"Is that it?" Hannah whispered.

The flashing neon light said everything. Joe's Love Me Tender Chapel O' Love. Lightbulbs formed a giant red heart on the roof, with an arrow of white slashed through it.

Their cabdriver from the airport had insisted on returning to chauffeur them, saying his wife was out of town and he had the evening free. The cynical half of Ross wondered if he got a kickback for every couple delivered to the chapel door, but it was an unworthy thought.

"Carlo" had taken them to the courthouse—also open until midnight—then turned the meter off while they got the license. He was enthusiastic about the joys of marriage and having *many* bambinos, exuding a refreshing earthiness in the midst of neon and glitz.

Hannah sat staring at the license with an expression that could only be interpreted as terror. Ross wanted to reassure her, but some of that same terror was stomping around his gut as well. The last time he'd made a trip down the aisle he'd ended up in divorce court and in the middle of an ugly custody battle.

Of course, he didn't need to worry about it with Hannah. She wasn't anything like Doreen. If he'd married someone like Hannah in the beginning, he might feel different about marriage.

"I'll be one of your witnesses," Carlo offered cheerfully. He cleared the trip meter and smiled when he saw Ross watching him. "Wedding present," he said simply.

They trooped into the chapel—which looked almost like a normal wedding chapel inside—but had to wait for the couple ahead of them.

"Ohmigod," Hannah breathed when she saw the bride emerge—the red leather mini was nearly obscured by a biker's jacket, and her hair looked like it had been styled by a squirrel in heat. The groom, on the other hand, was dressed in shorts, a tank top and safety pin earrings.

And his nose was pierced.

Hannah shrank back against Ross's broad chest and gulped. Well, at least she didn't need to worry about looking out of place in her jeans.

Ross put his arm around both her and Jamie. "This is nothing," he whispered in her ear. He was warm and reassuring and a little amused. "You haven't seen the minister yet."

Chapter Five

"Welcome, welcome," said a vaguely familiar voice.

Hannah turned her head and her jaw dropped in shock. It was Elvis in his nightclub days...or at least a five-foot-six, one-hundred-and-ten-pound version of Elvis, in head-to-toe sequins and fringe.

"These are my friends, Joe," Carlo exclaimed, giving his wife's second cousin an effusive hug. "You must marry them and sing something special."

"Happy to. Verrah, verrah happy."

Hannah pinned a smile on her face. Elvis? In her worst moments she'd never imagined being married by an Elvis look-alike. Not that Joe looked much like Elvis Presley, but he was trying so hard, it didn't seem polite to notice the obvious differences.

The uncertainty she'd felt from the beginning came back in full force. It was wrong to marry a man she didn't love, but how could she refuse? Ross needed her to protect his claim to Jamie, and Jamie needed a mother. She was so deep in thought, she didn't notice Ross trying to get her attention until he literally shook her shoulders.

"Uh...yes?" Everyone's eyes were focused on them and she swallowed. "Did I miss something?"

"Excuse us for a minute." Ross took her arm and dragged her into the chapel. "Are you having second thoughts?" he demanded.

"Me?" I'm about to get married by an Elvis impersonator, to a man who doesn't love me, Hannah added silently. What could possibly be wrong with that picture? Maybe they weren't truly going to be husband and wife, but marriage was special and sacred and she felt like a fraud, especially with Carlo enthusing about the joys of wedded life and having babies.

Something twinged deep in Hannah's abdomen at the reminder. She wouldn't be having any babies, but she'd have Jamie. And Doggit. She could mother a jittery cat and one little boy, and that would have to be enough.

"Why would I be having second thoughts?" she asked.

"You..." A growling sound came from Ross's throat.

Hannah smiled faintly. "You sound like a bear."

"I'm serious."

She glanced toward the door and saw Joe and Carlo in the outer room, watching with undisguised interest. They had an unspoken agreement not to say anything to spoil Carlo's pleasure in the proceedings. He was so sentimental, he'd be shocked by their practical arrangement.

"All right. What about you?" she asked softly. "Don't you feel strange about what we're doing?"

Ross sighed and raked his fingers through his hair. He couldn't blame Hannah for having doubts. "Of course, but whenever I see you and Jamie together, I know it's right. Why can't friends have a better marriage than all those people who think they're in love? What we have will last a lot longer."

"You really think love is *that* unimportant?"

A small voice in the back of his mind told him to be careful. Hannah had probably never been hurt by a lover; she didn't know what kind of damage it could do to your soul. If nothing else, he could protect her from that kind of pain.

"Well, there are different...kinds of love," he said, stumbling over the words.

Terrific. You're so profound, McCoy. He wanted to convince her to marry him, not conclude he was a walking cliché.

Her forehead creased. "What is that supposed to mean?"

"Friendship is a kind of love, isn't it? And we both love Jamie. So we're not so different from the other people who get married here."

Hannah crossed her arms over her chest and lifted her eyebrows. She looked him up and down, then shook her head decisively. "I don't think you're the type for a pierced nose and safety pin earrings, so I wouldn't compare myself to the other people who get married in Joe's Love Me Tender Chapel O' Love."

Ross laughed and pulled her to him for a hug— when all else failed he could count on Hannah's sense of humor. "You're right. Thank God for the small favors. Shall we go ahead then?"

"We've come this far, we might as well go all the way."

All the way... Ross whistled at the image it brought to mind. She didn't mean anything by her innocent statement, yet he had an instant vision of their bodies entwined on the king-size bed in their hotel suite.

And hugging her was definitely a mistake. He could still smell the fresh scent of her shampoo, and feel the soft curves of her breasts and hips against him—prompting distinctly *un*platonic sensations. He pushed the thought away with angry impatience. He didn't want to feel desire for Hannah. A man could be friends with a woman without sex coming into the picture.

Couldn't he?

"Is everything okay?" asked Carlo when they stepped back into the foyer. "You didn't argue, did you? You still want to get married?"

"Of course. It's just wedding jitters," Hannah said easily. "I'm sure Elvis understands. He must have seen a lot of nervous brides."

The minister swelled with pleasure at the use of his alter ego's name. "I sure have, young lady. Now I need to see your license and go through some paperwork, then we'll be all set."

The paperwork wasn't complicated—so many people got married in Reno, they had the process down to a fine science.

"Will it be a double-ring ceremony?" Joe asked last, and Ross shook his head.

"Nope, but I have one for Hannah." He leaned down and gave Jamie the gold band they'd gotten earlier. "Hold on tight, Tiger. When I ask for it, you give me the ring."

Jamie nodded and curled his small fingers around the circlet.

Just before they started, Ross went out to the taxi and retrieved the box he'd left there, carrying it back into the chapel. Hannah had looked at it curiously when they first headed for the courthouse, then seemed to have forgotten it. Feeling a little awkward, Ross opened the box and pulled out a bunch of flowers. It wasn't a formal wedding bouquet—more like the wildflowers Hannah used to pick and bring to school. Now he wondered if he should have gotten a traditional bouquet.

He cleared his throat. "They don't really look like forget-me-nots, but it's the closest I could get. I know they used to be your favorite."

Hannah stared at the bouquet of blue delphinium for a full minute. To his horror, tears filled her silver-green eyes and spilled down her cheeks.

"Hannah," Ross said, appalled. "I didn't mean... I'm sorry."

"No." She sniffed and took the flowers, touching them lightly with the tips of her fingers. "I'm just surprised. I didn't think you'd remember."

He didn't know if she meant about him remembering to get flowers for the wedding, or about what flowers she used to love. "Of course I remember the forget-me-nots," he said, deciding to stick with something safe. "You were crazy about them."

"I still am."

Carlo gave him an approving thumbs-up gesture, and signaled to someone inside the chapel. "Jamie is your best man, and I will give the bride away," he declared. "I have only sons—now is my chance to be the papa." He hustled Ross and Jamie to the front by the alter, then hurried back to take his place next to Hannah.

Ross caught Hannah's eye and they both smiled. Their wedding was being orchestrated by a Latin romantic with the subtlety of a starving grizzly. Nonetheless, Carlo was a good-hearted man who radiated an endearing ingenuousness.

The traditional wedding march swelled into a crescendo as Carlo escorted Hannah down the ten-foot aisle, beaming as proudly as her own father would have.

Their witnesses were Carlo, and Joe's wife, who ran the Blue Suede Shoes Hamburger Palace next door. When the bride and groom didn't have their own witnesses, Betty headed over to contribute her part to the festivities—the deluxe ceremony even included a free nuptial dinner at the Blue Suede Shoes. And last but not least, the receptionist doubled as a photographer.

Ross was glad he'd chosen the deluxe package. This was either the wedding-from-hell, or the funniest thing that had ever happened to him. At any rate, it was worth remembering.

When Joe came to the part about the ring, Ross took it from Jamie's small hand and looked at the gold circlet for a second.

This was it.

The big commitment. He was doing something he'd never expected to do again. But with Hannah it would be different, she didn't have a devious bone in her body.

"Place it on her finger and repeat after me...." Joe prompted.

Ross took Hannah's hand and stroked his thumb across her skin. He should have felt panicked, sliding the ring over her finger, but he didn't. When he'd thought Hannah was backing out of the marriage, *that* was when he'd panicked.

"With this ring, I thee wed," he said, a curious satisfaction in his heart.

The rest went in a blur, except when Joe invited him to kiss the bride. "Hello, Mrs. McCoy," he murmured, cupping Hannah's face between his fingers. "I never thought I'd say that to my Honeycomb, but I'm really glad it happened."

Pink stained her cheeks and he smiled. Hannah was his wife, and he would never have to wonder where she'd been, or who she'd been *with.* She understood commitment. And though a kiss wasn't necessary under the circumstances, he suddenly wanted to kiss her very much.

"I've never seen a woman blush so much," he whispered.

"It's my Scandinavian blood," she whispered back. "I'm so fair, it shows up more."

Maybe, maybe not. Ross thought it had mostly to do with her sweet, generous nature. Hannah had never gotten cynical or blasé about life.

He bent down, intending to place an affectionate kiss on her lips, but what started out casually slipped out of control with alarming speed. Tarnation. The restaurant... He should have remembered the restaurant and that kiss he'd started to keep her from denying their engagement.

Sometimes his brain was on vacation.

Ross pressed his hands against Hannah's back, arching her to him. The heck with his brain, it was the rest of his body that needed help.

"Daddy, Daddy, I want to hug Hannah, too." The

insistent voice and hand yanking on his jeans were more effective than a splash of cold water.

He pulled away, steadying his new wife as she blinked in shock. "Yes," Ross said hoarsely. "You can hug Hannah now."

Holy cow.

Hannah put her fingers to her lips, certain they'd been singed. It was hard to think with her blood still humming, but she instinctively knelt next to Jamie and accepted his enthused hug.

"Now you're my mommy, right, Hannah?"

"That's right."

Little boys were easy to handle; it was the grown-up ones she didn't understand. Like that kiss. Why would Ross kiss her so…enthusiastically? She looked up, saw him chatting with Carlo and made a face. As kisses went, it probably wasn't anything special to Ross, he was so experienced.

Her mouth tightened and she squared her shoulders. Okay, so Ross McCoy had more experience with *some* things. But she'd bet a hundred dollars he couldn't bake a pie, sew a shirt or even build a fire the way she could—a real fire, that is. Obviously there were other flames he could kindle without half trying.

"Such a beautiful wedding," Carlo exclaimed. "My wife would have cried and cried."

They signed their names a couple more times and received a ceremonial marriage certificate intended as a special keepsake. A stack of Polaroid pictures were slipped into a small plastic album, and they were finally able to climb back into the cab, having officially become a family.

Hannah turned the gold band around and around on her finger and stared out at the dark sky. There were so many lights from the town, the stars didn't have a chance to shine.

"Tired?" Ross asked. He shifted Jamie and slid closer to her. "It's been a big day."

"We didn't sleep much last night," she said quietly.

"No, but we can sleep later tomorrow. Our plane doesn't leave that early."

"Uh-huh."

Ross cupped the back of her neck and massaged her tight muscles. "You got awful quiet all of a sudden. Is something wrong?"

Hannah bit the inside of her lip. Talking wasn't a good idea right now; there was too much to think about. "No. Reno is just a bit overwhelming," she muttered. "It's interesting, but I'll admit to being out of my league."

It was partly true. Everything about Reno made her feel like a country bumpkin. The city had more bells and whistles and lights than a fireworks show. She preferred the quiet peace of Quicksilver, though it might be interesting to visit other places once in a while.

"I think you're doing fine, and if you wanted to see the casino, we could—"

"No," Hannah said quickly. She'd just taken the biggest gamble of her life, how could a few slot machines compete? "Let's just put Jamie to bed, and get some rest ourselves."

"Okay."

He didn't say anything else, and even Carlo seemed subdued. When they reached the hotel Ross tried to pay the fare, but Carlo would have none of it—he'd been lonely with his wife out of town, and seeing such a nice couple get married was a treat. He drove off with a friendly wave.

To Hannah, the hotel didn't look any quieter at ten in evening than it had several hours earlier. Holding the flowers Ross had given her, she followed him to the elevator and pushed the button to their floor since his arms were filled with a sleepy little boy.

In their suite she helped Jamie into his pajamas and tucked him into bed.

"G'night, Mommy," he said, having trouble talking between wide yawns. "G'night, Daddy."

"Good night, Tiger."

Hannah sat next to Jamie and waited until he fell asleep. She knew Ross planned to sleep in the room with his son, and she would use the second bedroom. It was all very neat and friendly, and she shouldn't mind. But she did. Dreams of happily-ever-after-love were darned stubborn.

The wedding ring felt strange, and she twisted it around her finger. The salesman at the hotel jewelry store had tried to sell them a diamond solitaire, but she'd chosen a simple gold band instead. Oh, Ross would have gotten the solitaire, or even the channel set diamond band she'd secretly admired, only, under the circumstances she'd wanted something less...conspicuous.

Though the blankets weren't wrinkled, Hannah smoothed them absently. She wasn't surprised Ross wanted her to wear a ring, but he'd obviously never thought about getting one for himself. She knew some men didn't like jewelry, yet her father had never taken his off, even after her mother's death.

Rings are for men in love, her head reminded. But

deep in her heart, Hannah still wished Ross had gotten a wedding ring to wear.

Someone knocked on the suite door and Hannah heard a murmur of voices. With a last kiss on Jamie's cheek, she slipped out of the room.

"Who was that?"

"The hotel management." Ross held up a silver bucket holding a bottle, and a single long-stemmed pink rose. "And there's a card, addressed to you."

Curious, she took the small envelope and read the note aloud. "'To the lovely new bride.'" Hannah wrinkled her nose and shook her head. Dropping onto the plush couch, she stretched out her legs and closed her eyes. "If getting married in Reno is this exhausting, I can't imagine what a fancy wedding must be like."

Ross frowned. "I think the note and rose are nice."

"Yeah, they probably send roses to all the new brides."

He took the note and read it again. There were several signatures and someone had sketched a heart with a flower in the middle. It was too personal to be nothing more than a formal hotel nicety.

"No, they sent the rose because they liked you," he said, thinking how everyone had gathered around Hannah when they registered. Granted, some of it was pure male attention for an attractive woman, but attractive women walked into hotels every day without drawing that kind of notice.

"That's sweet," Hannah said drowsily.

Sweet? A low noise came from Ross's throat. It was a sound he was beginning to recognize. Pure frustration. Hannah was intelligent, but she had a blind spot about herself. Most women didn't need anyone to tell them they were beautiful, but not Hannah. And some of it was his fault.

Ross sighed. He'd handled things badly. He wanted to keep their relationship on a platonic level, but he'd stumbled along the fine line between friendship and attraction.

And he was still stumbling.

He sat next to Hannah and traced a strand of hair clinging to her forehead. She murmured something indistinguishable and her eyes opened. "Yes?"

"I just wanted to make sure you were real," he said.

"Don't I look real?"

She looked better than real. When they'd first walked into the suite that afternoon, she'd stood under the air-conditioning vent and splashed water on her face. Moisture had trickled into the valley between her breasts and she'd looked flushed and pretty and so desirable he'd had trouble keeping his hands to himself.

Ross's fist clenched at the memory, then his fingers relaxed and he touched her hair again. What would Hannah do if he kissed her a second time, the way he'd kissed her at the chapel? They'd made an agreement about their marriage, but he'd also left it open to change. It might not be so bad, enjoying some of the usual marital comforts.

Lord in heaven…what was he thinking? Ross shifted backward on the couch and took several deep breaths. He didn't want to destroy their friendship.

Hannah watched him with a questioning frown between her eyes and he twisted his mouth into a smile.

"Hey…I know what you said about getting some rest, but it isn't that late. Let's use the hotel's baby-sitting service, and spend a couple hours downstairs.

I'm no gambler, but I can show you how to play roulette.''

"Mmm." She thought about it, then shook her head. "I don't want to leave Jamie with a stranger."

Ross nearly suggested she go downstairs alone, then changed his mind. Little could happen at the hotel— a discreet security staff kept things quiet and safe— but in a place like Reno, innocence was an aphrodisiac. He trusted Hannah, he just didn't trust the men who would try to pick her up.

"You go," Hannah said softly. "You're probably bored."

With me.

The unspoken words hung in the air and he gritted his teeth. "I'm not bored, I just wanted you to have some fun. This is our wedding night and there ought to be something special about it."

"I see. As opposed to a traditional wedding night?" She kept her eyes focused on the opposite wall, and Ross shook his head. An uncomfortable thought was stomping around his chest, mostly having to do with *how* innocent his new wife actually might be.

"Uh…Hannah, you *did* go out before. Right?"

"Go out?"

"On dates. How many men have you dated?"

"Dates?" She turned her head. "You know better than that. People don't date in Quicksilver, they go fishing and hiking. They work on the leaky roof of the church and laugh at the tourist who got goosed by a tree branch and thought it was a bear attack. Pretty soon they've spent so much time together they figure they might as well make the arrangement official."

"That didn't answer my question."

She sighed in defeat. "*Okay.* Exactly who would I

date? Bucky Lomax? He's only missing a *few* marbles. Or how about Arthur Stevenson? He's fifty-eight and thinks aliens have landed whenever the northern lights are visible. And there's always Toby Myers. A fifty-two-year age difference isn't *that* important when you're really in love.''

''You haven't ever...that is, you're a...?'' Ross stuttered into silence.

''A virgin? Is that what you're so delicately trying to discover?''

''Sort of.''

Hannah scowled at him. ''Well you can 'sort of' drop the subject. I'm not interested in discussing it any more.''

''You should have told me.''

''Why? What possible difference could it make?''

He vaulted to his feet and paced the room. ''It makes a lot of difference. I assumed you had some experience, that you knew what you'd be getting into.''

''What I'd be getting into?'' Hannah tossed her braid over her shoulder and glared. ''I'm not 'getting into' anything, remember? What you really mean, is whether I knew what I'd be giving *up*.''

To his shock, Ross felt an embarrassed heat crawling up his neck. Was blushing contagious? He didn't know what to do with a virgin wife. It wasn't what he'd expected, though he should have realized the possibility from the beginning. Hannah wouldn't have had any opportunity for romance in Quicksilver, not between raising her brothers and the lack of eligible men.

''I'm sorry,'' he muttered.

''For what?'' she shot back.

''For everything. But I still wish you'd told me.''

"Really?" Hannah got up and angrily walked toward her bedroom. "We may be buddies, but that isn't the sort of information I'd volunteer out of the blue. And since you want a strictly platonic marriage, I don't see that it's any of your business."

Hannah wanted to slam the door behind her, only it might wake Jamie, and she didn't want him to know they'd been fighting. She sank down on the mattress and tapped her fingers on the bed.

Her own vanity was getting in the way, but for the life of her, she couldn't understand why Ross gave a hoot about her being a virgin. It was probably one of those silly masculine things that didn't make any sense. Men could be so unreasonable.

Hannah kicked her shoes off so hard, they hit the opposite wall. The resounding *thud* made her smile.

She wasn't a wimp and she wasn't backing out. They might have an unconventional marriage, but she was Ross's wife and Jamie's mother now, and that counted for a lot. Anyway, their arguments never lasted very long; in the morning everything would return to normal and they'd go back home to Alaska.

Right. Hannah crawled into bed and tried to sleep, yet it felt awfully lonely listening to the shower run in the other room. She had a brief, tantalizing vision of Ross standing naked under the stream of water and groaned. She'd always considered herself a reasonably intelligent, sane individual, but that was before she'd gotten married.

There was no way around it. A woman who agreed to a platonic marriage with a man like Ross McCoy was just plain crazy.

Chapter Six

"**G**ood morning." Hannah walked out of her bedroom and smiled sunnily.

Ross warily looked at his new wife. "Good morning."

"Is Jamie awake?"

"No, he's still sound asleep and hogging the bed. Yesterday was pretty tiring for a kid that age, and it's also an hour earlier at home."

"Yup." Hannah took a piece of toast off the tray he'd ordered from room service and munched it.

For the life of him, he couldn't tell what she was thinking and it was driving him nuts. She seemed to have gotten more sleep than he'd accomplished, though it wasn't surprising. *Hannah* wasn't the one who'd acted like a Grade A jerk; that was purely his own doing.

"Is there anything special you'd like for breakfast?" he asked, watching her drift to the window and look out. "They have a good menu here."

"Toast and coffee are fine." Hannah stretched like a lazy cat. "But Jamie needs something nutritious. Does he have any special preferences? And I need to know if he has any allergies."

Business as usual? She was acting like nothing had happened, and he couldn't stand it any longer. "Aren't you going to say anything?" Ross demanded.

"About what?"

"About last night. About what we were talking about. I don't know—about anything."

She grinned and shook her head. "Let's put it down to stress—you were freaked about getting married again, and I was in culture shock. Reno is overwhelming for someone who's always lived in Quicksilver. But we never stayed angry when we were kids, and we shouldn't change that now."

Jeez, that was annoying. He would have felt much better if she'd slapped his face or yelled at him, so he focused on the first part of her speech. "I wasn't freaked."

"No?"

"No." Ross could tell she didn't believe him, but it was easier than admitting he'd let his body get the upper hand the previous evening. Obviously, kissing Hannah was a mistake; she had the unfortunate effect of making him forget they were just friends.

She watched him a while longer, then shrugged. "Okay. I'll go check on Jamie. I think he's waking up."

With another friendly smile, she walked into his bedroom. As she leaned over the rumpled bed in her tight jeans, Ross clenched a fistful of hair in his fingers and pulled.

Why was it, now that he'd gotten exactly what he

wanted, he had this insane impulse to change the rules?

"We're home. What do you think?" Ross asked. He'd gotten out of the truck and stood waiting for her reaction.

Hannah sat and stared at the house. She'd imagined something similar to the age-worn homes in Quicksilver, only this was very different.

They'd driven through a thick spruce-hemlock forest, but the house sat in a natural clearing—a solid two-story building built of unweathered yellow logs and flanked by comfortable porches. Just a few years old, the structure looked perfect in the meadow with the mountains rising beyond it.

Ross held out his hand. "We'll give you the ten-cent tour."

She still wasn't accustomed to his courteous gestures, but she accepted the helping hand and climbed from the truck. It didn't mean anything special, she reasoned; Ross probably always acted that way with women.

Their flight back to Alaska had been uneventful, with Jamie talking nonstop, telling everyone on the plane that Hannah was his new mommy. She'd almost gotten used to people looking at them and smiling at the boy's enthusiasm. Ross was quieter, watching her with thoughtful eyes.

"Come on." Jamie dragged her to the front door. "I have my own room and Daddy gave me a whole set of trains with whistles and steam and tracks with bridges. We play with them a lot."

Hannah cast a glance at Ross. "We? So you finally got your train set."

His embarrassed grin made her laugh. Years ago, a nine-year-old Ross had set his heart on a train set in a mail-order catalog. The McCoys didn't have money for that sort of thing, but he'd faithfully saved his pennies. Then by the time he'd saved enough, his interests had shifted to full-size planes.

"Having a son is like having a second childhood," he admitted. Before going inside he took down a note taped to the door and read it. "It's from Callie and Mike. They said they put your things in the storeroom, and that Doggit is fine—he's upstairs in one of the bathrooms. Probably sulking," Ross added, "from being left alone all night."

"Hmmm...*oh.*" They'd just stepped inside and Hannah's eyes widened. A lot of Alaska homes were built with small windows to conserve energy, but the roomy interior of Ross's house glowed with mellow wood tones and natural light.

"Sealed, triple-paned windows," Ross explained. "They make it more practical."

"That's great."

Though Jamie was anxious for her to go upstairs and see his train set, he waited while his father showed Hannah the first level of her new home.

A large living room and dining area dominated one corner of the house, with polished wood floors, big, comfortable furniture and a sunken area near the fireplace. The modern kitchen had appliances Hannah had never seen except in a catalog, with broad counters and a shiny blue potbelly stove for heat.

Ross adjusted a stack of dirty dishes on the table. "I guess things got out of hand," he muttered.

Hannah swallowed at the understatement. The stove was the only shiny thing in sight—nobody could accuse Ross of being a great housekeeper. No wonder he wanted to get married, he couldn't *pay* someone enough to clean this place.

"Uh...this is my home office in here," Ross said quickly, as if to distract her.

She didn't say anything, just followed him. The rest of the downstairs area consisted of the office, a pantry, utility room and a couple of empty bedrooms.

"I thought you might pick one of these rooms for yourself," Ross said, looking around the largest. The floor-to-ceiling windows afforded a breathtaking view of the meadow and mountains. "This is supposed to be the master bedroom, only I never bothered to set it up. There are also a couple of extra rooms upstairs if you'd prefer something else."

Hannah bit her lip, longing to ask if he'd lived here with Doreen. He'd probably say it wasn't important, but things like that *were* important, to a woman at least.

"The house seems large for a bachelor," she said slowly.

Ross lifted a quizzical eyebrow. "I commissioned the design quite a while back, but didn't get around to building the place until a couple years ago. I wanted Jamie to have a real home. Doreen dragged him all over the place, and when it got too inconvenient, she'd park him with friends or relatives," he said, too softly for his son to overhear.

"Inconvenient?"

A grim smile twisted his mouth. "Yeah...it got *real* inconvenient when one of her boyfriends didn't like having a kid around."

"Then why did she fight you on the custody issue? It would have been easier to just give him up."

He glanced at Jamie, then met her gaze with an intense expression. "Why else? She didn't want to give up those fat child-support payments I was sending."

Hannah's heart ached for the pain Ross had gone through, yet he clearly didn't want her sympathy. She looked away and ran her palms over her thighs. "I...uh, like this room," she said. "It's lovely."

"Then it's yours. I picked up a bedroom set in Anchorage last week, and I'll set everything up later. Now you should go see Jamie's trains."

She nodded, at the same time chewing over the piece of information he'd let slip. *I picked up a bedroom set in Anchorage last week....* Was he so certain she'd marry him that he'd gone ahead and ordered furniture for her bedroom? Her *separate* bedroom?

Arrogant wretch. Hannah gritted her teeth.

They climbed the back staircase, with Jamie chattering happily away. The trains were a child's fantasy, with every imaginable accessory. Jamie showed how the engine tooted and raced around the track, and how he could make steam come out when his papa helped.

As the engine went around the complex route for the third time, a frantic meowing led Hannah to the bathroom when Doggit waited. The feline launched himself into her arms, rubbing his face on her jaw and kneading the front of her shirt with his paws.

Ross leaned against the doorjamb and envied the cat's paws— they were precisely where he'd like his own hands to be. He'd decided it was natural to feel moments of desire for Hannah. He didn't enjoy wanting her, but there wasn't any point to denying what he felt.

"Jamie, I want you to meet Doggit," Hannah called. She carried the cat into the playroom.

Feline and child regarded each other suspiciously, but it turned out that Doggit was fascinated by Jamie's trains, which cemented their friendship. He crouched next to Jamie and watched the engine circling the track, his whiskers twitching with nervous intensity.

After a few minutes, Hannah climbed to her feet and dusted her hands. "I'm going to work on the kitchen," she said. "We're in danger of being declared a health hazard."

Ross winced. Until he'd looked at the house through Hannah's eyes, he hadn't realized how bad things had gotten. "It's my mess. I'll take care of it," he said quickly.

"No...you get my bedroom set up. I'd hate to see that new furniture you bought go to waste."

He paused for a heartbeat. Hannah's face was composed, a light smile playing on her lips. Yet every instinct he possessed told him she was annoyed, and not about dirty dishes. "Does that mean something?"

"Nothing at all." Hannah slid past him and marched down the hallway.

He whistled and slouched against the wall. His plan for a comfortable marriage between friends was going to hell in the proverbial hand basket.

It didn't matter whether sex was in the picture or not—obviously a buddy stopped being a buddy once she became a wife.

Hannah shoved her hands in a pan of soapy dishwater and glared out the window. It was silly to be angry, but her pride was taking a severe beating from this marriage.

PLAY
RUN
FOR THE
ROSES

and get
THREE FREE GIFTS!
HOW TO PLAY:

1. With a coin, carefully scratch off the silver box at the right. Then check the claim chart to see what we have for you — **2 FREE BOOKS** and a **FREE GIFT** — **ALL YOURS FREE!**

2. Send back the card and you'll receive two brand-new Silhouette Romance® novels. These books have a cover price of $3.50 each in the U.S. and $3.99 each in Canada, but they are yours to keep absolutely free.

3. There's no catch. You're under no obligation to buy anything. We charge nothing — ZERO — for your first shipment. And you don't have to make any minimum number of purchases — not even one!

4. The fact is, thousands of readers enjoy receiving books by mail from the Silhouette Reader Service™. They enjoy the convenience of home delivery...they like getting the best new novels at discount prices, BEFORE they're available in stores... and they love their *Heart to Heart* subscriber newsletter featuring author news, horoscopes, recipes, book reviews and much more!

5. We hope that after receiving your free books you'll want to remain a subscriber. But the choice is yours — to continue or cancel, any time at all! So why not take us up on our invitation, with no risk of any kind. You'll be glad you did!

Visit us online at
www.eHarlequin.com

This surprise mystery gift
Could be yours **FREE** –
When you play
RUN for the ROSES

Scratch
Here
See Claim Chart

YES! I have scratched off the silver box. Please send me the 2 FREE books and gift for which I qualify! I understand that I am under no obligation to purchase any books, as explained on the back and opposite page.

RUN for the ROSES	Claim Chart
♔ ♔ ♔	**2 FREE BOOKS AND A MYSTERY GIFT!**
♔ ♔	**1 FREE BOOK!**
♔	**TRY AGAIN!**

NAME   (PLEASE PRINT CLEARLY)

ADDRESS

APT.#   CITY

STATE/PROV.   ZIP/POSTAL CODE

315 SDL C246

215 SDL C242
(S-R-OS-05/00)

The Silhouette Reader Service™ — Here's how it works:

Accepting your 2 free books and gift places you under no obligation to buy anything. You may keep the books and gift and return the shipping statement marked "cancel." If you do not cancel, about a month later we'll send you 6 additional novels and bill you just $2.90 each in the U.S., or $3.25 each in Canada, plus 25¢ delivery per book and applicable taxes if any.*
That's the complete price and — compared to cover prices of $3.50 each in the U.S. and $3.99 each in Canada — it's quite a bargain! You may cancel at any time, but if you choose to continue, every month we'll send you 6 more books, which you may either purchase at the discount price or return to us and cancel your subscription.

*Terms and prices subject to change without notice. Sales tax applicable in N.Y. Canadian residents will be charged applicable provincial taxes and GST.

If offer card is missing write to: Silhouette Reader Service, 3010 Walden Ave., P.O. Box 1867, Buffalo NY 14240-1867

BUSINESS REPLY MAIL
FIRST-CLASS MAIL   PERMIT NO. 717   BUFFALO, NY

POSTAGE WILL BE PAID BY ADDRESSEE

SILHOUETTE READER SERVICE
3010 WALDEN AVE
PO BOX 1867
BUFFALO NY 14240-9952

NO POSTAGE
NECESSARY
IF MAILED
IN THE
UNITED STATES

"He got the furniture last week. A whole *week* before he proposed," she mumbled beneath her breath, scrubbing at an oatmeal-encrusted pot. Flipping the water on, she rinsed the pot and put it in the crowded drainer.

Of course, Ross had decided on separate bedrooms *before* he'd seen her again, so that should make her feel better, not worse. And her head kept saying it was a compliment that he wanted her to be his son's mother.

If only her heart was convinced.

A black-tailed deer browsing in the meadow put his head up, warily scenting the air. Hannah watched the wild creature, admiring its instinct for survival. People weren't always so careful and it got them into trouble. Like now...she couldn't decide if she was in serious trouble, or just adjusting to a new environment.

"Do you like the house, Honeycomb?" Ross asked from behind her.

Startled, Hannah rinsed her fingers and turned around. "It's great." She didn't add it would be much better when she removed a few layers of dirty laundry, dishes and outdoor equipment that belonged in a storage room, rather than all over the house.

He grinned ruefully, apparently reading her mind. "I'm really sorry about the way things look. I'm usually neater than this, but with Jamie..." He shrugged. "We're still adjusting. We can hire a housekeeper if you'd like."

"That's all right." She smiled, unable to stay upset when Ross had that little-boy apologetic expression on his face. "But it'll take a while to figure how everything works—outside of a Sears catalog, I've never seen appliances like this," she confessed, having decided it would be silly to pretend she knew what she was doing.

"Such as?"

"Such as a dishwasher, food processor, and that… whatever it is." Hannah pointed to an odd looking machine on the center island. "I touched something on the front and it made a terrible racket."

"That's my espresso maker—you must have pushed the button that starts the coffee grinder. Do you want a cup?"

She shook her head. "No. But do you have any instruction manuals? I'm not kidding about never seeing this stuff before. You know what Quicksilver is like—they still think television is a newfangled invention."

"I remember." Grinning, Ross opened a drawer and pulled out a sheaf of booklets. "Everything you need is right here. Call me if you have any questions. I'll be fixing your bedroom."

Whoa.

The grin sent quivers to the bottom of Hannah's stomach and she nearly threw the booklets at his departing back. Why couldn't Ross have turned out to be a geek? The kind of guy a woman wanted to give a puppy-dog pat on the head, not crawl into bed with.

And she'd *agreed* to it. That was the worst part. She couldn't even blame alcohol or a bump on the head for her lapse in judgment, just Ross's sexy smile and his devotion to Jamie.

He's your friend, remember?

Remember?

Right, like she could forget. Hannah plopped into a chair at the table and shoved the booklets down with the dirty dishes. She treasured her memories of Ross and their friendship and didn't want to lose it. Even after all these years they still felt the same bond of affection, though her feelings were getting complicated by sexual attraction. Maybe if they'd stayed in contact it wouldn't be so strange now; she could have adjusted to his growing sex appeal without overdosing on it.

But *noooo*, this was like going seventeen years without candy and then suddenly moving into the Hershey's chocolate factory. Who could blame her for feeling befuddled?

It might be easier, sleeping farther away from Ross. Her imagination wouldn't get out of control if they didn't stumble across each other going in and out of the bathroom. The master bedroom had a lovely private bath of its own. After sharing a single bathroom with six brothers and her father, it would be nice to enjoy plenty of hot water and a little privacy.

Except...the downstairs bedroom was a long way from Jamie. Hannah jumped up and flew into the room where Ross was working.

"This can't be my bedroom," she said.

Ross finished screwing two pieces of the frame together, then looked up. "Why not?"

"Jamie. I can't hear him down here."

"No problem. That's what baby monitors are for. I bought a couple when I got Jamie. I even use one upstairs."

A small frown creased her forehead. She'd heard about baby monitors, of course. They worked like portable walkie-talkies—you put one in the child's room, and the other next to your bed.

"I don't know. Are you sure I'll be able to hear him?"

"Yup. You can turn the volume way up, even hear him breathing if that makes you feel better."

He bent over the furniture he was assembling and Hannah swallowed. She'd seen men working before, but they didn't have Ross McCoy's body—it was nearly perfect, with broad shoulders, a flat stomach, long, powerful legs and a killer backside. For years she'd wondered why women admired a man's buns, and now she knew.

"Anything else?" he asked without looking up.

"Uh…no."

She backed out as quickly as she'd come in, suddenly unsure if her objections had anything to do with Jamie. Maybe she subconsciously wanted to sleep closer to Ross, and Jamie was her excuse.

Taking a calming breath, Hannah surveyed her new home. It was a disaster through and through, but underneath was a beautiful, well-designed house. It was decidedly masculine, but she could fix that. Heck, she could fix practically anything, so the house didn't have a chance.

She just wished she felt the same about her marriage.

In the bedroom Ross heaved the mattress onto the frame and scowled. He was glad Hannah had picked the downstairs bedroom. *Really* glad. It was part of his plan all along.

Of course, Hannah would still come upstairs to tuck Jamie into bed, but he wouldn't have any uncomfortable encounters with her. No towels slipping and exposing feminine parts of the body. He wouldn't smell her shampoo or fantasize about being invited to share her shower.

This whole marriage was working out the way he wanted.

Really.

"Hannah?" Ross called.

"Yes?" Hannah looked up from the oven she was cleaning and blew a strand of hair from her face. The self-cleaning cycle of the stove was a modern miracle, but the designer had probably expected it to be used occasionally, not ignored. "You're home early," she said.

The past five days had passed uneventfully. They were settling into a routine that was calm and peaceful, and downright *boring*.

No. She shook her head. Not boring, just placid. Ross was working extra hours to make up for his absence, and she was busy removing dust and washing dirty laundry. It wasn't any wonder he owned a fortune in household appliances, he needed all the help he could get.

"You're early," she said. "Dinner isn't ready."

"Good. Callie invited us to eat at their place, so you won't have to cook."

Hannah hesitated. She'd been dragging her feet about meeting Callie Fitzpatrick. They'd talked briefly on the phone. Hannah had thanked Callie for taking care of Doggit and getting her things from Quicksilver, and Callie had apologized about not having time to do something with the mess in Ross's house.

Do something? Callie would have needed ten hands and a month to "do something" with the mess. All in all, the other woman sounded very pleasant, but Hannah couldn't forget Ross's enthusiasm about her on the day they were married.

"What's wrong, Hannah? I thought you'd want to be friends with Callie," Ross said, exasperated. "You have all kinds of things in common. And she invited Donovan Masters for dinner, too. I told you about Donovan—he's the third partner in Triple M Transit."

"I want to meet her, but I've been busy."

"You've been working too hard," he said bluntly. "The house looks great, but you don't have to do everything in the first week. I didn't marry you just to clean house."

"All right." Hannah stood up. She'd have to meet Callie sooner or later. "But I hope they don't dress up for dinner."

"Nope. She said to come any time, so get ready and I'll take care of Jamie."

He disappeared out the door and Hannah leaned against the stove. It would be nice to get out and meet some of the people around Kachelak, she assured herself. And she'd heard plenty about Mike and Callie and Donovan. They had to be nice people or Ross wouldn't be friends or business partners with them.

She tried to keep those assurances in her head while she showered and dressed in a clean pair of jeans and a shirt, but they weren't much comfort. Heck, she'd *seen* a picture of Callie—the woman had red hair, sex appeal and a husband who adored her. What could they possibly have in common?

You're just afraid Ross will compare you to Callie.

Hannah made a face in the mirror and acknowledged that was exactly what she was afraid of. It was illogical and unfounded, but her feelings about Ross weren't too logical these days.

"Let's go, Mommy," called Jamie from the living room.

"I'll be right out." Hannah stopped in the kitchen and wrapped foil around the blueberry pie she'd baked earlier. Ross hadn't said to bring a contribution to the meal, but it seemed a proper thing to do.

Unlike Hannah, Jamie was excited about having dinner with the Fitzpatricks. They'd barely arrived at the other couple's home when he started jumping up and down. "I get to tell Callie and Mike," he declared.

"Tell them what, Tiger?" Ross asked.

"About my new mommy."

Hannah laughed and let herself be pulled toward the house. Each day Jamie crept deeper into her heart, making her feel warm and loved and needed. Whenever she worried about the decision she'd made, his hugs and kisses made it go away.

Ross followed his son and wife, carrying the blueberry pie she'd insisted on bringing. He sniffed at an opening in the foil and hoped Hannah would bake another one soon. They'd only been married for a few days, but he was already getting spoiled by good cooking and clean clothing.

But he didn't understand why she was so reluctant to meet Callie. He knew they'd hit it off. In the ways that mattered, they were just alike.

The door opened and Callie stepped out. "Hi, Ross, Jamie…and you must be Hannah. I'm so glad to meet you."

"She's my new mommy," Jamie announced quickly.

"That's wonderful." She ruffled the child's hair, then tucked Hannah's arm into hers. "Come inside and we'll talk. You can tell me stories about Ross when he was a kid and I'll tell you some about Mike.

Then we can spend the evening teasing our husbands."

Hannah looked back and lifted her eyebrows.

Ross coughed uncomfortably.

"Sounds like fun," Hannah agreed. "How much do you want to embarrass them?"

"Lots," Callie assured her.

Mike clapped Ross on the shoulder in a gesture of shared condolence. "This could be dangerous. Callie's been really looking forward to your coming—she knew she was going to love Hannah when she met Doggit."

Ross leaned toward his friend and lowered his voice. "Isn't that the ugliest cat you've ever seen? And Hannah is just crazy about him."

"Yeah, but you haven't been dumb enough to say so, right?"

"Are you kidding? I'm smarter than I look."

A burst of laughter came from their wives, already chatting furiously away.

Mike grinned. "It's no secret I don't agree with your reasons for getting married," he said candidly, and Ross nodded—Mike had been extremely vocal with his protests. "But I'm glad Callie and Hannah can be friends. Callie is used to more people than we have around here and I'm afraid she'll get lonely."

"You're not having problems, are you?" Ross asked.

His friend shook his head and grinned. "Not a chance." Mike had only been married for three months and he still had the cockeyed expression that newlyweds got.

Most newlyweds, Ross reminded himself.

His marriage to Hannah was based on a more practical and solid foundation, with no chemical combustion to confuse them. The silent lie made him uncomfortable and he gritted his teeth. He was doing his best to avoid any combustion with Hannah, so it was *still* different from Mike and Callie's marriage.

"Here," he said, thrusting the pie at his partner. "It's blueberry. Hannah thought we should bring something—I guess it's a feminine thing."

Donovan Masters uncoiled himself from a chair and stole the pie from Mike. "Man, this isn't fair. You both got women who can cook. By default, I should get to take this home with me."

"You could get married, too," said Callie as she carried a steaming casserole dish into the dining room. Hannah followed with a bowl of salad and a basket of French bread. "No one is forcing you to stay single."

"Nope, I'm going to be the hold-out. Someone has to strike a blow for bachelorhood."

Mike folded his wife in an embrace. "You're just jealous because Callie wanted me instead of you."

"I never had a chance, she was determined to marry you before she ever arrived in Alaska. You dazzled her when she was just a little girl."

"Lucky me."

Hannah watched Callie and her husband with a twinge of envy. The love that flowed between them was almost palpable—a passionate, tender bond that made her throat ache. And from the gentle way Mike stroked his wife's stomach, Hannah knew a big announcement was coming. Callie was pregnant.

How could Ross *not* believe in love when he saw a man and a woman so plainly devoted to one another? The question occupied her mind, even as she ate dinner and visited with the others.

Though she'd been reluctant to meet Callie, it was impossible to dislike any of Ross's friends; they were genuinely interesting people who enjoyed each other's company. Hannah was a stranger, yet they were willing to accept her presence because of Ross and Jamie.

After the meal they went into the living room and Mike smiled knowingly. "Now you're in for it, Hannah. Callie loves getting a new victim she can bore with our wedding pictures."

Callie punched him lightly in the arm, but she laughed and eagerly grabbed a white album sitting on the coffee table. "Well…since Mike already raised the subject, I might as well."

Hannah obligingly took the album and pored over the photographs, made compelling by the Fitzpatricks' shimmering happiness. Ross and Donovan were also in the pictures, along with a number of people Callie explained were Mike's family and her father.

"You'll have to see my wedding album, too," Hannah said, glancing mischievously in Ross's direction.

"Oh?" Callie murmured. They'd talked about a number of things, but she'd conspicuously avoided the subject of Hannah's marriage.

"Oh, yes. We were married by Elvis Presley at the 'Love Me Tender Chapel O' Love.'"

"Elvis?" Mike sounded as if he'd been strangled. "You were married by Elvis? How romantic."

Ross sent a murderous glare toward his friend. Mike didn't approve of his marriage, and this would be one more strike against him. "We had a friendly cabdriver who recommended his cousin for the wedding."

"His wife's second cousin." Hannah beamed. "Imagine having a cabdriver related to Elvis. You know, the King isn't as tall as I expected, but his voice is as good as ever.''

Ross stared at his wife. Could Hannah really be so innocent and sheltered she didn't believe Elvis was dead? It was possible. Quicksilver was removed from the world, isolated in more ways than its geography.

"Uh…Hannah," he said. "You know that wasn't actually Elvis Presley, right? He was an impersonator.''

Hannah blinked. "Of course. *Everyone* knows Elvis works out of Las Vegas, not Reno.''

He froze for a full thirty seconds, then his wife and friends burst out laughing.

"I take it all back," Mike said between chuckles. "You two are perfect for each other.''

Chapter Seven

Ross was silent on the drive home.

Hannah had laughed and joked about her wedding, yet memories of a teenage Hannah kept floating through his mind. Sweet Hannah, dreaming of walking down the aisle in the tiny church in Quicksilver. Hannah, saying she'd fill the church with flowers and wear her mother's wedding dress.

He'd forgotten all that.

Maybe he'd wanted to forget. He couldn't do anything to make her dreams come true, because her biggest dream had been to fall in love. The most he could offer was friendship.

Hell, he might as well admit it. He'd rushed Hannah to Reno so she couldn't change her mind about marrying him. Now he regretted that hasty decision. Mike had given Callie her dream wedding, full of romance and love and family, and he'd given Hannah...Elvis.

"Bath time, Jamie," Hannah said when they got

back to the house. "Then you can play with your trains for an hour before bed."

"Yippee!" Jamie scrambled up the stairs. "Can Doggit take a bath with me?"

"Doggit wouldn't like that," she said, following him. "He cleans himself with his tongue, remember?"

Despite his inner turmoil, Ross grinned. Jamie's first bath with Hannah had ended with everyone wet and laughing...everyone except Doggit. An ill-timed splash of water had sent him fleeing from the scene, hissing and spitting with every step. Doggit now avoided Jamie's bathroom as if a pack of wolves lived there.

"You're awfully quiet," Hannah said once Jamie was busy playing with his trains. "I didn't think you'd mind being teased."

"No." Ross shook his head. "But let's go downstairs, I want to talk."

"Sure."

In the living room she sank onto the couch, tucking one leg beneath her. The green flannel shirt she wore was soft from washing and he was surprised how feminine it looked on her. But then, he was discovering everything about Hannah was graceful and feminine.

"I *don't* believe Elvis Presley is alive," she said. "If that's what your grim expression is about. I just couldn't resist pulling your leg."

"I know. I'd be worried if you didn't tease me."

"So what's wrong?"

Ross cleared his throat. "Nothing's wrong... exactly. But I've been thinking about our wedding."

Hannah looked surprised. "What about it?"

"You always wanted to be married in Quicksilver."

She shrugged and tapped her finger on the soft leather of the couch. "That was a long time ago. Hopefully I'm a little more practical now."

Lord, she wasn't helping one tiny bit. He wanted to know if she regretted their hasty, ridiculous wedding in Nevada, and she was talking about becoming more practical. A woman could be practical and still have romantic dreams.

Ross shook his head to clear it. "You were never *im*practical. You took over the family at fourteen— including caring for a newborn baby. It takes common sense to raise kids at that age."

"Thanks," she said dryly.

This wasn't going well.

"I'm just saying you have a sensible approach to life."

"That's me, sensible Hannah." She stood and straightened the cuffs of her shirt. "Now that we have that settled, I've got some things to do."

"No, it's not settled," Ross growled. Obviously he would have to use the direct approach. "I want to know if you regret getting married so quickly. We could have had the ceremony in Quicksilver. Maybe we should have."

Hannah shook her head and laughed. "I'm not like Callie. I don't expect things like that."

"What do you mean?"

"I'm just like not her. She's the kind of woman who has a beautiful, fancy wedding."

"And you're *not* that kind of woman?" His voice shook and he tried to get a grip on his temper, though he was mostly angry at himself.

"Ross…" Hannah paused and flicked the tip of her tongue across her lips. "Don't worry about it. We both agreed to getting married in Reno, and it was the right thing to do. Besides, we would have felt silly doing it another way.''

"Yeah. Right. As opposed to *not* feeling silly in Joe's Love Me Tender Chapel O' Love?''

"Exactly.''

Hannah wasn't quite sure what Ross was getting at, but she was anxious to end the conversation. Why bother about Reno now? They were married—sort of—and that was that.

"I have some laundry to do,'' she said. "But I'll go up and tuck Jamie into bed when he's done with his play time.''

Ross nodded without seeming to pay attention.

"Well...okay.'' Hannah turned and headed for her bedroom. Inside, she shut the door and scowled with all her might. She could hardly get within ten feet of Ross without having hot flashes and uncomfortable cravings, and he thought she was sensible.

"Sensible,'' she muttered.

Swell.

"Women." Ross whacked his hand into the couch and growled wordlessly. He didn't need to ask why Hannah thought she wasn't "like Callie,'' it was obvious.

She didn't have any experience with men and she had a crazy notion she wasn't desirable. At least, she didn't think she was desirable to him.

Not desirable?

Ross groaned, thinking about the cold shower he'd taken on their wedding night. He'd been upset about their argument, but his concern about her being a virgin was purely bogus—he'd realized it the second she disappeared into her room. The idea of making love to Hannah and knowing he was the only man who would touch her... It darn near drove him insane.

No, Hannah wasn't the problem, *he* was the problem.

His reasons for wanting a platonic relationship were rooted in his past, not in her appeal as a woman, yet everything he did seemed to make things worse.

Life and friendship sure got complicated when you weren't kids anymore.

In the past few days he'd discovered more about his wife than he'd ever bargained to learn. Hannah was amazing—she had a natural, uncomplicated sensuality unlike any woman he'd ever known. But it wasn't just sexual; it was the way she savored the small pleasures, like petting her cat, or stretching in the morning or licking a drop of syrup from her lip.

And he loved the way she loved Jamie.

Doggit drifted into the living room, meowing plaintively.

"I have a big problem," Ross said to the cat. "And since we both males, you'd probably understand."

"Mrrowww." Doggit lay down and curled his paws beneath him.

"Or maybe not. I'll bet you're the love 'em and leave 'em kind of guy, right? You don't worry about falling in love and getting your heart chopped up."

The feline's eyes narrowed into slits and the tip of his tail twitched irritably.

"I'm really losing my mind, talking to a cat." Ross dropped his head back and called himself a couple of names. Without meaning to, he'd added to Hannah's lack of confidence. She was so special, and she didn't seem to know it.

So…what if he tried to show her?

Ross sat up and looked around the room—it wouldn't be hard creating a romantic setting. He wanted Hannah to understand how beautiful she was—that's all. It had nothing to do with needing to touch her, or finally kissing her the way he wanted. Surely he could keep things under control.

Yet a nagging question bothered his conscience. Was this just the excuse he'd been looking for?

After tucking Jamie into bed, Hannah slipped down the back staircase and out to the back porch. The brisk chill of the evening penetrated her shirt, but she just rubbed her arms, reluctant to go back inside.

She knew she was avoiding Ross, but she didn't see any point in discussing their wedding. The truth was, it wouldn't be any different if they'd gotten married in Quicksilver. Mike and Callie's wedding was beautiful because they were in love, not because of white lace and orange blossoms.

Very simply, she and Ross were friends. And if she let her attraction to him get out of control, she could ruin their friendship.

Breathing deeply, Hannah focused on the wild land beyond the house. Moonlight illuminated the small meadow, and the faint gurgle of a nearby stream filled the night with a quiet music…until the porch creaked behind her. Her attention was instantly confined to the man standing a few feet away.

"We should have a good frost soon," Ross said. "Maybe tonight, according to the radio."

"I know." Hannah gritted her teeth. *Now* he wanted to talk about the weather? Why couldn't he have gone straight to weather and bypassed "sensible"? She was really starting to hate that word.

Ross stepped closer. "I built a fire."

"It should keep the house warm for the night. But I have to admit, I appreciate your central heating," she said.

"*Our* house, *our* central heating," he emphasized.

Hannah swallowed. *Our house...* What a lovely thought. The houses in Quicksilver had all started out as homesteaders' cabins, with successively added rooms and patchworked twentieth-century amenities. Livable, if not terribly comfortable. But Ross's house was perfect, a modern Alaska home that blended functionality with a rugged sophistication. It was a lot like Ross.

"I'm glad you like the house," he said simply.

The sharp cracking of a stick caught his attention and he scanned the area beyond the porch. The large, lumbering shape of a bear paused in a pool of moonlight twenty feet away, lifting its head and sniffing the air.

"Shhh," Ross whispered.

Hannah rolled her eyes. She'd dealt with brownies all her life. You had to be careful, but since they weren't hiding peanut-butter sandwiches in their pockets, and hadn't gotten between the bear and a T-bone steak, they were reasonably safe.

After several minutes of casting his nose about in the slight breeze, the brownie ambled on, accompanied by more rustling leaves and breaking branches.

"He comes by every night," she murmured.

Ross looked at Hannah, a perplexed frown between his eyes. She sounded entirely too calm, but after a moment he laughed to himself. Of course. That was one of the reasons he'd married Hannah; she was an Alaskan woman, prepared to deal with life in the frontier state. It would take more than a disinterested grizzly bear to worry her.

"Every night, eh?"

"Yes. He limps. That's how I can tell it's the same one. Poor thing. He must have tangled with a trap or something."

Considering his bulky size and power, Ross didn't think the bear needed any sympathy. His gait might have been uneven, but he was hardly crippled.

"Let's go inside…sit by the fire," he suggested.

Her shrug was barely perceptible in the shadows. "I don't know. It's late. Maybe I'll just go to bed."

Damn. She wasn't making this easy.

"Wait a while," Ross coaxed. "I opened that bottle of champagne we were given in Reno…from the hotel management. We didn't get a chance to drink it."

"You brought it back?"

"Of course." He put his hand on her waist and pulled her closer. "I should have toasted my lovely wife on our wedding night, but instead I stuffed my foot in my mouth."

"I'm not lovely."

"You're wrong," Ross said with more force than he'd intended. He sensed Hannah's confusion, but she needed to understand the way he saw her—as a beautiful, desirable woman.

Each misunderstood word and dismissed compliment would build a wall between them. It had to stop. He didn't want Mike's kind of marriage, but he wanted the warmth and laughter he'd always shared with Hannah. The way things were going between them, they'd end up as angry strangers, not friends.

Taking her hand, he laced their fingers together. He'd known she went outside after putting Jamie to bed, absorbing the rhythms of the night. For the last three evenings he'd watched from a darkened kitchen, aching with the beauty in her slender body. She was like a wild falcon, alert to every scent and sound and sensation.

"Come inside," he said, drawing her into the house.

Hannah's eyes widened when she saw the living room, transformed into a place of intimate shadows and flickering candlelight. The champagne sat next to the couch in front of the fireplace, along with two goblets.

"You—this is nice," she whispered.

"You deserve most of the credit," Ross said easily. "It's so much cleaner now. How do you keep ahead of Jamie's toys and clothes and everything?"

"Practice." Hannah intended to sit on the opposite end of the couch, but somehow she'd ended up next to him. "Lots and lots of practice. I cleaned up after six brothers—who were major slobs—for most of my life. But it wasn't all Jamie's things, you know."

Ross glanced around, his forehead creased thoughtfully. "Yeah, it looks terrific. I can't put my finger on what's different, but something."

She bit her tongue, thinking of the boots, skis, kayak paddles, fishing gear and other sports and outdoor equipment she'd moved to a proper storage place. Ross probably *was* neat as he'd claimed...in a masculine, who-cares-what-it-looks-like-as-long-as-I-can-find-it sort of way.

He handed her a fluted glass filled with sparkling golden liquid. Her first taste of champagne. It ought to be interesting, though it looked like ginger ale.

"To our marriage," Ross said as he held his own glass out and she obligingly clinked hers to his. "And to my wife," he added.

Hannah swallowed experimentally, bubbles bursting inside her mouth and throat. Mmm... Champagne might look like ginger ale, but it didn't taste like it. She cast a surreptitious glance at Ross.

"You've been avoiding me," he said. "People who are married should talk."

"I'm not avoiding you. I've been busy." She drained the rest of her champagne, then frowned at the empty glass. "Anyway, we talk at breakfast and dinner."

"I know, but Jamie is always there."

"Yes," Hannah muttered. "Jamie is the reason we're married."

"Not exactly."

She twisted and stared at Ross. "What do you *mean*, not exactly? You wanted a mother for Jamie. A wife to show the court in case of a custody battle."

"I wouldn't have married just any woman. And if I hadn't gone through such misery with Doreen, I might want a very different relationship with you."

The room tilted and Hannah wondered if she could be drunk on a single glass of champagne. Maybe it affected you more when you weren't used to alcohol. She stole another glance at Ross. He looked serious and intent, and the expression in his eyes practically curled her toes.

"That's...interesting."

He smiled faintly. "You have no idea how interesting. I've had a terrible time keeping my hands to myself. That's why I thought we should discuss it—

you've probably gotten some mixed messages from me.''

He took her glass and poured more of the champagne. Hannah's hand shook when she took it, and some of the wine spilled onto her fingers and dripped to his thigh.

''Sorry,'' she said, embarrassed.

''No problem.''

Hannah forgot to breathe when Ross lifted her hand and drew his tongue over her wet skin. The velvet warmth of his mouth sent tendrils of fire through her veins.

''It tastes better this way, like honey from a honeycomb,'' he whispered. Setting the glass aside, Ross brushed her cheek with his palm. ''It reminds me of when we got to Reno. The afternoon was so hot, and you weren't used to the heat.''

She could barely think, much less know what Reno's desert heat had to do with anything, but she nodded jerkily. ''Y-yes?''

''You splashed water on your face to cool off.'' His fingers trailed down her throat. ''It rolled down... here.'' Ross stroked the opening of her flannel shirt. ''I envied that water—it was in such a sweet place.''

She searched his face, trying to understand what he was thinking, but his eyes were intent on her breasts. She gulped, unaccustomed to anyone looking at her so...blatantly.

Ross groaned at the feel of Hannah's smooth skin. He eased his hand under the fabric of her shirt and she shivered. A reaction to his touch? He enjoyed that idea an awful lot, so he experimented, delving farther until his fingers rested on the curve of her breast. His thumb made several lazy circles and she shivered again, though he couldn't tell if it was from fear or a more agreeable emotion.

"You're lovely," he breathed, swiftly sliding buttons from their holes. More than anything he wanted to strip the cloth away, to see more of the bounty beneath.

"Women are pretty much the same," she said with a touch of defiance. She squirmed a few inches away and caught the lapels of her shirt together. "We all have the same fundamental equipment."

A low, hoarse chuckle escaped his throat. "Oh, Hannah. You have no idea what you're saying."

"Sure, I'm making you laugh. I'm a riot a minute." Hannah's bleak tone made Ross frown.

"Sweetheart—"

"Don't call me that," she snapped.

"Why not?" he asked calmly. "We can't act like strangers, Hannah. We've known each other all our lives. I'm just trying to clear the air, so we both know what's going on."

"Nothing is going on. You made it perfectly clear what you want from this marriage. And how could I take it personally? You got new furniture for my bedroom before you ever came back to Quicksilver—everything decided before you ever saw me again."

Ross gritted his teeth, but his frustration faded when he saw a reflection of deep hurt in her silver-green eyes. "I don't understand," he said, choosing his words with care. "That should make it clear my decision had nothing to do with you."

"It has a lot to do with me," she muttered. "You didn't even think it was *possible* you'd change your mind. Heck, I'd never gotten married, so I couldn't be very desirable. Right? I'm just sensible ol' Hannah, Quicksilver's resident old maid.''

"Honeycomb..." He stopped. This was a case of men and women looking at things in different ways. They were friends, but she was also a woman who wanted to feel beautiful. "I never thought you weren't desirable. Remember how shocked I was when you said you were a virgin?"

"*You* said that, not me."

Ross wanted to watch Hannah's face, to gauge her reactions, yet it was difficult to keep his gaze from lingering on her lush curves—high, full breasts above a narrow waist and gently flared hips. And her scent, purely feminine, without any expensive perfume to hide the enticing fragrance.

Honeycomb.

It wasn't an innocent nickname anymore, not when he was haunted by the thought of tasting her.

"You...uh..." He cleared his throat.

"I don't want to talk about this anymore," Hannah said rebelliously.

Sighing, Ross decided it was time for a more direct approach. Without giving her time to object, he swept her onto his lap. "Keep still, woman," he muttered when she squirmed.

"This isn't funny, Ross."

His fingers locked on her hips. "Neither is what you're doing to me," he muttered. "I can't... Oh, *hell*." He tipped her backward and pinned her to the couch.

Stunned into silence, Hannah stared at Ross.

"Do I have your attention?" he growled.

He definitely had her attention.

"All right. Remember in the restaurant? How it felt when we kissed? How *I* felt?"

The soft rasp of a zipper barely registered in her consciousness, but there was no mistaking his hand tracing her belly button, then sliding lower against bare skin. "I don't...know what you're talking about," she gasped, her lungs desperate for air as he massaged her abdomen. Sensation spread from the caress until she felt it in every part of her body.

"Think about it."

How was she supposed to think when he was touching her like that? Hannah moaned softly and shifted her legs, trying to ease the aching hunger he'd created.

She wasn't entirely certain she liked the sensation of losing control, or of being at the mercy of her senses. Everything seemed heightened—the dance of candlelight on the walls, the warmth radiating from the fireplace...the solid heat of Ross's body.

"What's wrong?" Ross slid more fully on top of her, and she jerked as his fingers settled over her breast.

"Nothing."

"Good." His thumb circled her nipple, teasing and coaxing it into hardness. Tiny stabs of electricity shot through Hannah's blood and she forgot to breathe.

No.

She didn't know what he was playing at, but she'd just lie here and pretend it wasn't affecting her in the slightest. Only, she couldn't, especially when his mouth settled over the same sensitized peak, warmth and moisture seeping through the fabric covering it.

Her abdomen clenched and unclenched and she grabbed a handful of Ross's hair, but instead of pull-

ing, her body arched of its own accord, holding him
to her.

"Hannah, you're making me crazy." His hip
pressed into her thigh and she squirmed; something
felt funny...something not quite right.

*Remember in the restaurant? How it felt when we
kissed? How I* felt?

Think about it.

The restaurant, his odd expression when she'd
jumped from his lap. The insistent pressure beneath
her bottom. What was it she'd read once...a man
wasn't built like a woman, so they couldn't disguise
their response in certain situations?

Hannah gulped.

She'd observed enough of animals in their natural
setting to know exactly what that bulge meant, and it
wasn't a lack of masculine interest. She didn't have
any measurement to judge by, but even with her lim-
ited knowledge it was obvious that Ross was more
man than most.

"Ross?"

"Yes? Ah, there it is."

Her thoughts were definitely mushy, so she didn't
know what he meant at first. But when his fingers
caressed her again, she jumped in startled recognition.
The cotton barrier of her bra had disappeared and she
was exposed to his gaze and touch.

Ross circled the tips of her breasts with his thumbs,
blew gently on the rosy peaks, then drew one into his
mouth with a deliberate care that arched her body off
the cushions. A pressure grew inside that was almost
frightening.

"Ah...Hannah," Ross moaned.

Her name.

There was enough sense in Hannah's head to be glad. He knew it was her, not a nameless, faceless woman. Nibbling kisses moved up her throat and Ross finally took her mouth in a seamless joining. His tongue stroked over hers, a velvet warmth that tasted of champagne. Her knees instinctively lifted, and he settled into the nest she'd made for him.

Ross thought he'd never touched any so soft as Hannah. She was all silk and heat, and he wanted her so much, it was burning him alive. Yet, as he slid his hand between their bodies to unfasten his jeans, he froze in shock.

What am I doing?

Chapter Eight

Ross braced his weight on his forearms and stared at Hannah. She lay on the cushions, her breasts pink and taut with his wild caresses.

"Ross?"

Her eyes had turned a turbulent green, all traces of silver erased by passion. Yet, doubt had begun to creep into their depths and she trembled.

"Don't move...just stay there." He didn't even recognize his own voice, it was so hoarse. What had started as an attempt to reassure her had gone out of control—he'd nearly made love to Hannah, and his body still screamed for release within her sweet warmth.

"What's wrong?"

"Nothing. *Everything.* I shouldn't have let it go this far." With a painful groan he rolled away and sat on the floor, trying to gain some command over his arousal. "I'm sorry, it was a mistake."

With shaking fingers Hannah gathered her shirt over

her breasts and tried to make sense of what was happening. Yet the only thing her brain could process were Ross's last words.

It was a mistake.

A mistake.

Kissing her was an error in judgment. Anger simmered deep in her chest and she struggled to sit upright.

"You're right, it was a mistake," she said in a brittle tone.

"I just wanted you to know how beautiful you are," he muttered. "I didn't mean to get carried away."

Still shaking, Hannah fastened the front clasp of her bra, then thrust a shirt button back through its hole. "I presume this has something to do with me being more inexperienced than you expected, right?"

He didn't say anything, staring instead at the bright flames in the grate.

"Well, thank you very much, but I don't need you to play Prince Charming to my Sleeping Beauty," she snapped.

"That's not what I was trying to do." Ross turned his head and looked at her. "And I don't mind about you being a virgin. It shocked me, that's all. Hell, I'm relieved you don't have the habit of hopping into other men's beds."

Hannah took a quick breath. "I see. Did Doreen...?"

"I was never sure, but she gave me plenty of reasons to wonder. She didn't like to be alone, and I was frequently out of town on business. I felt like a damned fool when she walked out so soon after we were married."

"That doesn't mean she wasn't faithful."

Ross gave her a hooded glance from the corner of his eye. "No, but when she asked for child support her lawyer handed me the evidence I'd need to confirm my paternity. It was pretty obvious what it all meant."

The stark fury in his voice made Hannah want to reach out to him, but she knew he wouldn't want her sympathy. This wasn't a matter of friendship, it was a matter of pride. She knew a lot about pride, especially since hers had been abused recently. Not that Ross had ever intended to hurt her, but as the saying went, the road to hell was paved with good intentions.

"No one could doubt Jamie belongs to you," she whispered. "You look so much alike."

Ross nodded. "I don't have doubts about my son, but it's my fault he has a mother who uses him for her personal gain. And it's all because I couldn't see beyond Doreen's pretty face and body. Love confuses things... You can't see the truth even if it's staring you in the face."

Hannah's fingers clenched around the tails of her shirt. Ross wasn't talking about love, he was talking about lust, and they were two different things. She didn't need a hundred sexual encounters to understand such a basic truth.

"Ross..." she said helplessly.

"Forget it." He climbed to his feet and looked down at her for a long minute. "Good night, Hannah." Without waiting for a response, he turned and headed for the staircase.

Good night?

She glared at his departing back. So, the subject was closed because Ross had decided they didn't need to discuss it any longer.

The wretch.

Men thought they knew everything.

Rocking from side to side to ease the lingering ache of desire in her stomach, Hannah pulled her legs up and rested her chin on her knees. The fire burned on cheerfully and she scowled at the flames.

Her head wanted to understand why Ross acted the way he did, but her heart and body were just plain angry. And frustrated. Intellectually she understood why he didn't want an intimate relationship, but it was impossible to forget the way she felt when he touched her. It wasn't just the touching, it was the little things—like Ross holding a door for her, or his smile, or the way he protected Jamie. He had a compelling, gentle strength, unlike any man she'd ever known.

Doggit jumped to the back of the couch and delicately pawed at Hannah's shoulder. Sighing, she straightened her knees to give him a place to sit. He settled on her lap and gave his leg a cursory lick.

"I agreed to this marriage," she said softly, not really talking to him.

The feline laid his chin on her hand and closed his eyes. He knew when he wasn't needed in a conversation.

"Ross didn't sugarcoat things when he proposed to me. He was very straightforward and honest." Hannah's fingers moved in Doggit's fur, finding comfort in his silken warmth.

The solidly built house usually didn't permit the sound of footsteps from the second floor, but upstairs Hannah heard a distinct double thud from the direction of Ross's bedroom.

His shoes?

Hannah stirred restlessly, imagining each piece of clothing Ross might be removing—shirt, jeans…

underwear. She'd felt his bare chest against her skin
and the memory lent tantalizing detail to the process.
The shower came on and she pressed her lips together.
Marriage without love or passion? Ross might have
been honest about his wishes for their marriage, but
she personally thought it was nuts.

You haven't been hurt, like he was.

No, she'd never been hurt. Romance was a scarce
commodity in Quicksilver. Logically, she knew she'd
never married because her family needed her. It was
a commitment she'd accepted with few regrets.

Of course, no one had ever come along and *tried* to
change her mind about that commitment, either. Hannah smiled ruefully. It was natural to have occasional
doubts about her appeal as a woman, but that was *her*
problem, not Ross's.

"He has a lot of nerve," she muttered, getting annoyed again. "Thinking he can kiss me and then just
brush it off. I could swear he felt something, so why
did he stop so abruptly? It's like I suddenly grew tentacles or something."

Was she so unappealing to Ross? Being a virgin
didn't mean she was ignorant; men didn't usually call
things off after a certain point, not with a willing partner. And she'd certainly been willing.

More than willing, darn it.

Heat flushed Hannah's body at the reminder. "Men
are rats," she mumbled. "They say women are difficult, but the male animal is the one who's irrational
and utterly impossible."

Doggit snored, oblivious to the insults being heaped
on his sex.

Hannah inched down until she lay flat on the couch.
It would have been worse if Ross only wanted a sexual

relationship, without friendship or warmth, she assured herself. She ought to feel lucky. Except she didn't feel lucky—she just felt alone, and aching, and wondering if she'd ever feel right again.

"Mommy?"

Hannah opened her eyes. Jamie stood over her, a worried expression on his face. "Yes?"

"Are you okay?"

She blinked and tried to clear her head. It was morning and something didn't seem exactly right. Rising on one elbow, she looked around and sighed—of course, she'd fallen asleep in the living room.

"It's all right." She swung her legs to the floor and gave Jamie a kiss. "I was enjoying the fire and fell asleep. That's all. Why?"

"'Cause Papa's grumpy." Jamie wrinkled his nose and snuggled into her arms. "Only, he says to never mind him."

"That's right, Tiger," Ross said from across the room. "I'm just a bear with a sore paw, so don't pay any attention." He stood near the door, dressed and ready to leave for work.

"I forgot you had that early flight," Hannah murmured. He was taking a load of fruit and vegetables to Kotzebue and wouldn't be back until late evening.

"That's all right," he said casually, but he didn't look like he'd slept well, and she worried about him flying without a full night's rest.

"Can't you wait for a few minutes?" she asked. "I'll make some coffee."

When he nodded, Hannah kissed Jamie again and hurried to the kitchen. She'd set up the coffeemaker the night before, so it was a simple matter to flip the switch. While it was brewing she pulled sandwich makings from the refrigerator and swiftly prepared a lunch he could bring with him.

"That isn't necessary," Ross said. "I can manage."

"It's safer to have food and coffee with you. Especially on such a long flight."

Ross leaned against a counter and watched his wife's quick, efficient motions. On the two other mornings when he'd had early junkets, Hannah was awake before him, with a lunch to take and coffee already hot in a thermos. Obviously she'd planned to do the same this morning, but had forgotten after the previous evening's fiasco.

A man could get spoiled by that kind of attention. He was fortunate she had a forgiving nature, or he might have been eating at the local pizza parlor for a few days.

"Did you eat breakfast?" Hannah asked over her shoulder.

"No. I'll pick up something later."

"Later you'll be halfway to the Arctic Circle," she said, already breaking eggs into a skillet. "And don't tell me a box of doughnuts takes the place of a real meal. You can wait a few minutes. It won't make that much difference."

Ross turned a chair around and straddled it. He wasn't really in a hurry. He'd wanted to get out of the house before Hannah woke up, mostly to avoid awkward "almost-morning-after" questions. He wasn't proud of the way he'd handled things, yet fixing them seemed equally impossible.

"How do you know about the doughnuts?" he asked.

"Callie. She said you guys used to live on them."

"Callie has a big mouth."

"I'm telling her you said that." Hannah slid a plate onto the table along with a steaming cup of coffee.

"You wouldn't."

She lifted an eyebrow and Ross decided not to pursue the subject. Hannah didn't sit with him, as she'd done on other mornings, instead busying herself with his lunch. His fork grated on the plate as he looked at her. Barefoot, cheeks flushed with sleep, her hair rumpled the way it would have been if he'd taken her to his bed...she was a man's fantasy.

She had fastened exactly two buttons on her flannel shirt, over her breasts, and it barely concealed the part of her body he'd already seen to such advantage.

You're not interested, Ross reminded himself savagely. He'd never intended things to go so far between them. The thought of becoming obsessive over another woman sent cold chills down his spine. Love was too much of a risk, even with Hannah.

He gulped down his breakfast, oblivious to her chiding that he was setting a bad example for Jamie.

"Jamie isn't in here," he muttered, swallowing the last bite and getting up. "I'll be in after midnight," he said. "So I'll see you tomorrow."

She kept her lips pressed together and handed him a thermos and the cooler containing his food.

"Thanks."

Hannah followed Ross as he headed to his truck. Over her protests, he'd bought her a Dodge Dakota to do errands with, and drive to the store. He had another truck, but he'd insisted she needed something new and more reliable for winter driving.

"Ross...about last night," she said hesitantly.

"You're getting chilled. Anyway, I don't have time to discuss it, Hannah."

His tone didn't invite taking the subject further, but she lifted her chin. "Why do I have a feeling you don't *intend* to discuss it? Ever?"

The sun was still below the horizon, yet despite the faint light, she could see him stiffen. "Because I don't. Just forget last night ever happened." Ross slammed the vehicle door and started the engine.

Just forget... How was she supposed to do that?

Hannah crossed her arms over her stomach and glared as the truck disappeared down the road. Only, it was frosty cold outside and she wasn't wearing shoes, so she finally turned around and went back into the house. Jamie had fallen asleep again, on the couch with Doggit curled up with him.

How long would it be before the tension between the adults in his life began to affect him? He worried about things no child should have to worry about. But she didn't know how to fix it, especially if Ross wouldn't talk to her.

She watched Jamie for a long while, letting a measure of contentment fill her at the sight of his sweet face. Jamie McCoy was her son; there was no hesitation in her love for him. He was the son she would like to have given Ross.

At the thought of carrying Ross's baby something twinged deep in her abdomen, and Hannah fled to the kitchen. He frustrated her in so many ways, yet her heart was getting more and more involved in this marriage. And her body. Her body was definitely lobbying for more involvement. Kissing Ross was like eating chocolate-chip cookies—once you've eaten one, you're hooked for life.

Millions of men and women got married, had a family *and* managed to stay in love. Love and marriage went together, like ham and eggs or fish and water.

What was wrong with wanting it all?

Ross parked by the house, weariness riding his shoulders like a heavy weight. They usually made deliveries to the Arctic Circle an overnighter, sleeping in the plane to make things easier. But he hated to leave Jamie, even for a night.

And Hannah, his conscience whispered.

It was true. He hated to leave Hannah, and the knowledge ate at him. Each time he'd taken a sip of coffee or eaten a bite of the sandwiches she prepared, he'd thought of her, and his body had tightened with response. It was far more powerful and complex than what he'd felt for his first wife, and that worried him.

Lights shone on the porch and in the house, a subtle reminder of his wife and her caring ways. It was all so new, having a woman act like that. Doreen had never made an effort in the months they were married, and he'd grown up in a masculine household with no feminine frills.

A grim smile touched Ross's mouth as he recalled his father, saying how lucky they were not having to deal with a woman's foolishness. Whistling in the wind, because he couldn't do anything about it except get drunk and try to forget his delicate wife who'd died of pneumonia.

Sighing, Ross climbed the porch stairs and let himself into the house. The fragrant scent of fresh bread greeted him and he inhaled deeply.

"Rough flight?" Hannah sat on the couch, pulling a needle and thread through a piece of fabric.

"No, just long." Ross stretched, and a sense of peace crept into him. It wasn't logical, since life with Hannah was becoming more disturbing than peaceful. "What are you doing?"

"Mending."

He looked more closely and saw a basket spilling over with clothing. "Those are the rags I threw out in the garage."

She shook her head. "No, these are shirts and jeans and jackets that need buttons and seams stitched. There's no reason to get rid of them."

"That's right—you used to fix things for me," Ross said, recalling something from long ago. One day he'd gotten in a fight and torn his shirt. Hannah had insisted on mending it for him, so his father wouldn't be angry. After that, she kept a thread and needle and extra buttons in her school desk. In quiet, unassuming ways she'd always taken care of him.

She still was.

"Mending makes more sense than turning perfectly good clothing into rags," Hannah said, shaking out the garment she just repaired. "Are you hungry?"

"Yeah, something smells great."

In the kitchen Hannah filled a bowl with thick, meaty stew from a pot warming on the stove. She sliced a pile of fresh bread and sat next to him while he ate.

"I hope you didn't wait up for me," Ross murmured between mouthfuls.

Her shoulders lifted in a careless shrug. "It's no big deal. I used to wait up for Pop, too."

I'm not your father, he thought, then groaned silently.

No, he was Hannah's husband.

It was ironic. He'd married his old friend because she was the only female he trusted with his son, but he'd forgotten that little girls could grow into desirable women.

Hannah could tempt a saint, and he was just a man, something that was getting harder and harder to ignore.

Two mornings later Hannah hummed to herself as she ran an iron over a shirt. Ross was still sleeping and Jamie was playing, so she'd moved the ironing board to where she could work and look out the window at the same time.

Hannah hung the shirt on a hanger and took another from the basket. She'd scrubbed, vacuumed, polished and run the washing machine until the house shone. Now that everything was in order it wouldn't be as hard keeping it clean.

"No, Doggit," she said firmly, dissuading the cat from climbing into the basket of warm laundry.

"Mrrrow."

"Go sit by the door. There's lots of sunshine today."

Doggit plopped down in a pool of light pouring through the window. After a moment the warmth soaked through his fur and he began purring.

Hannah smiled at the feline, understanding his pleasure. Ross had chosen a beautiful place to build a home. A well-drained meadow invited wildlife from the surrounding forest. The mountains behind were moderately high and rimmed with a permanent frosting of white. They contained some respectable glaciers that Ross had promised they'd explore the next spring.

Ross... Drat him, she thought in sudden irritation.

He'd steadfastly refused to discuss that night they'd kissed, and it confused her more than ever. If he felt just friendship for her, how could he kiss her so intimately?

It didn't make sense.

And the more Hannah thought about it, the more she was certain he'd been really...*interested* in making love.

The object of her thoughts drifted into the kitchen, looking half-asleep, and her heart skipped a few beats. Dark beard shadow dusted his jaw, his jeans weren't snapped and a black shirt hung open exposing his chest.

"Coffee?" she asked.

"I can get it." He poured himself a mug and inhaled the scent before drinking. "Mmm. Your coffee tastes better than my coffee."

"I used to run a restaurant. I've made enough coffee to float the *Titanic*."

Ross frowned as he looked at her. "Most of your clothing looks worn-out. You have the checkbook and credit card, right? You don't need to ask to buy anything you want."

Hannah shook her head. "I have plenty, but the old stuff is softer."

She ran her fingers over the worn fabric on her thighs and Ross sighed. He had a healthy appreciation for Hannah's delicate skin; it haunted his dreams, both day and night. Yet he'd never been so contented. He would have eventually gotten things under control after getting Jamie, but Hannah brought more than domestic control to their lives.

"If you're hungry, there's oatmeal on the stove and

cinnamon rolls in the oven,'' she told him as she finished with another one of his shirts.

Ross pulled out the rolls and his mouth watered—homemade, stuffed with raisins and pecans, and dripping with brown sugar and cinnamon. ''It looks great, but you don't have to work so hard…do so much extra for us,'' he said guiltily. ''You need time for yourself.''

''What do you mean? What extra?''

He could tell she honestly didn't know, and a sense of wonder swept through him. It was just Hannah's way, doing for her family. And *he* was now her family, along with Jamie, reaping the benefit of her generous nature.

Friendship really *was* the best basis for a marriage, as long as he kept sex out of it.

''You're picking up that group of tourists today, aren't you?'' she asked.

''In Bethel.'' Sudden inspiration hit and he smiled. ''But Mike is headed for Anchorage. You should go with him. It only takes about an hour and you can go shopping for that stuff you wanted for the house.''

''It's not that important,'' she murmured. ''I'm used to doing without—Quicksilver isn't a shopping mecca, you know.''

''I know, I used to get real tired of mail-order catalogs, filled with things we didn't have money to buy.'' Ross stirred the oatmeal, surprised at the faint bitterness in his voice.

''But you made a success of yourself.''

''Yeah.'' He didn't add that his success had been a double-edged sword, attracting women like his exwife. ''Donovan and I have a lot in common. His mom was divorced and they didn't have much money, either.''

"What about Mike Fitzpatrick?''

"Mike?'' Ross popped a piece of cinnamon roll into his mouth and munched happily. "Solid middle-class. He came to Alaska for the adventure of the north and to escape from the kind of boring, conventional life his parents enjoy.''

Hannah laughed. "I see. That's why he married a girl from his hometown and is promptly starting a family.''

"Something like that,'' Ross said, grinning as well. "Actually, Callie turned out to be quite a handful, so Mike isn't complaining about boredom.''

"You really like her, don't you?''

There was an odd note in Hannah's voice and Ross frowned. "Callie is a friend, that's all.''

"Like we're friends,'' she said noncommittally.

The memory of Hannah lying on the couch, flushed with passion, filled his mind and he shifted in abrupt discomfort.

"Not exactly. We're…closer.'' It was such a flagrant understatement that he choked on his oatmeal. "Well, I'd better head for the airport. I want to check the engine before leaving.''

Her silver-green eyes were unreadable, but she nodded and set the iron on its base. "I baked cookies for your passengers and packed a lot of sandwiches—just in case anyone got hungry. And I used the two-liter thermos, so there's plenty of coffee.''

"Thanks.'' Unable to help himself, Ross caught Hannah's hand and looked into her eyes. "Honeycomb…I want you to be happy. You know that, don't you?''

Hannah swallowed, her skin tingling from Ross's touch. "Yes."

"I know I've been difficult, but it takes time to adjust to being married. We'll be okay, won't we?"

The worry in his face made her smile sadly. They were going to be okay, but she wanted a lot more than *okay*. "We'll be fine," she said. "Now go inspect your engine and have a safe flight."

He dropped a light kiss on her forehead. "Good. I'll see you tonight."

Hannah stared at her pile of ironing for a minute, not really seeing it. If things didn't change, they would settle into a comfortable pattern of polite morning conversation and kisses on the forehead. All right for friends, but she wanted more than friendship. A *whole* lot more. Sighing, she dropped into a chair and tapped her fingers on the table.

She'd fallen in love with Ross.

The realization had hit her around three that morning, but she doubted he returned the emotion. Even if Ross trusted love, she wasn't his type. Heck, there were plenty of snapshots around of his various girlfriends, women far more sophisticated and assured than she'd ever be. Of course, that didn't mean she couldn't change a *little*.

"I don't know anything about dresses and silk stockings and makeup," Hannah muttered. "Maybe I'm that 'type' and never had the chance to find out."

She thoughtfully ran her fingers across the worn fabric of her jeans. The softness pleased her, but they didn't look too great. And Ross *had* told her to buy something new.

Hannah rested her chin on her hand and gazed into the distance. She wouldn't let anyone dress her in something that didn't feel right, but Callie knew a lot about clothing and shopping and style. It wouldn't hurt to have expert advice on a shopping trip.

Before she could change her mind, Hannah reached for the telephone. She dialed the airport and prayed Ross wouldn't answer the call.

"Triple M Transit, may I help you?" said Callie's bright voice, and Hannah breathed a sigh of relief.

"Hi, it's Hannah Lig—McCoy," she said, stumbling over her new last name. "Has Mike left for Anchorage yet?"

"No. Did you want to go?"

"Uh…yes. And is there any chance you could come, too? I want to do some shopping."

"I'd love to," Callie agreed instantly. "What kind of shopping did you have in mind?"

A vision of silk nightgowns rose before Hannah's eyes and she blushed. "Some things for the house. And some clothing. Something special," she added.

"Sounds interesting. Are you going to a party?"

A private party.

Very private.

She drew a deep breath for courage. "Yes, something exclusive. In the bedroom, if I can convince him."

"That's wonderful." Callie's voice lowered to a whisper. "Does Ross have any idea about this?"

Hannah thought about the kiss they'd shared in front of the fire. Ross had an idea; he just didn't want to go anywhere with it. "He's been resisting. He doesn't want to talk about it."

"That's usually the stage when they're ready to explode and taking cold showers," Callie murmured, her tone laced with knowing amusement.

"Do you really think so?" Hannah asked hopefully. She didn't object to Ross taking cold showers because of her, as long as he didn't do it for the rest of their lives.

"Let's just say he's been on edge since you two got back from Reno. With Ross it's hard to tell, but I'm betting he's got more on his mind than flying tourists around the state."

"Good." Hannah smiled. "Jamie and I can be down to the airfield in a half hour. Do you think Ross will have left for Bethel by then?"

"He just lifted off. You're in the clear."

Hannah put the phone down and shivered with excitement. It was as if she'd been waiting for this moment her entire life, and didn't even know it. For a second she considered the idea she might have been in love with Ross all those years ago, then shook her head.

She'd been fond of the boy, but she loved the man. It was as simple as that.

Chapter Nine

"**I**s that me?"

Hannah looked at herself in the bedroom mirror and blinked at the transformation. It was still *her,* yet with some significant differences.

Her negligee was a silvery green with a matching nightgown. The deceptively simple outfit was long to the floor, of shimmering silk, and devoid of decoration except for the ribbon ties at the shoulders. But it clung in all the right places, and the plunging neckline revealed a disconcerting amount of her chest.

"Just let Ross call me sensible in this getup," she announced.

Outside, truck tires crunched on the driveway. Hannah checked the clock and saw it was after ten o'clock. *Perfect.* Jamie was sound asleep in bed, and it was late enough that she could legitimately be dressed for bed. Now all she needed was the courage to saunter out and pretend there wasn't anything unusual about the way she looked.

"Hannah?" Ross called softly. "Is Jamie asleep?"

Hannah's heart skipped a beat. If Ross didn't notice anything new about her she'd probably kill him, especially after going through her first trip to the beauty salon.

Adjusting the negligee to reveal the neckline of her nightgown, she walked into the living room. "He was a little tired," she said, her voice husky with both fear and excitement. "I decided to go to Anchorage after all, so it was a big day."

Ross turned and stared at his wife. "Hannah?"

"Yes?"

"You...uh. *Jeez.*" It was all he could manage. He'd left Hannah in the morning, and come home to a stranger.

"If you're hungry, I can fix a bowl of soup," she murmured.

"No." He might never eat again. "What happened...to your hair?"

Hannah lifted her hand and touched the shining length that just brushed the tops of her breasts, then shrugged. "Nothing much. I had it cut a few inches and highlighted. I like it...don't you?"

"Sure. It's great. Just great." He swallowed and decided to sit down.

It wasn't her hair, it was the revealing silk and seductive smile that shocked him. He was having trouble keeping his eyes on her face, especially with the way her nightgown molded her body. The fabric was so sheer, he could see the darker aureoles of her nipples, pressing against the fabric.

"Callie went, too," Hannah said. "You were right about us having a lot in common. I really like her."

He wondered briefly if Callie had talked his wife

into the new haircut and clothing, then dismissed the thought as quickly as it had come. Hannah made up her own mind, even if he didn't always understand her reasons and what she was thinking.

Like now.

He didn't have the foggiest notion what was going on behind her green eyes and it worried him. But other thoughts worried him even more—thoughts about making love to her. Or thinking it didn't make sense for two normal, healthy adults to get married and not sleep together.

Hannah smiled again and she took his breath away. "Jamie was an angel. I have to admit I'm not used to such good behavior from little boys. My brothers were somewhat wilder."

"Jamie has his wild moments."

"Yes. I wouldn't want him any other way." She knelt by the fireplace and struck a match. The carefully laid wood and kindling caught fire quickly, sending a cheerful light and warmth into the room. Ross shot to his feet, remembering the night he'd kissed Hannah.

"I think I'll go to bed," he said through clenched teeth.

"Are you all right? You seem stressed."

"Stressed" was an understatement. The pressure growing behind the zipper of his jeans was pure agony. He wanted Hannah more than he'd ever wanted another woman, and it was getting increasingly difficult to come up with reasons why he shouldn't make love to his own wife.

"I may be getting a migraine," he lied.

Guilt nagged him when her expression shifted from mysteriously sensual to concerned. "I'm sorry. Go upstairs and lie down. I'll make some tea. When Mother had migraines, she said peppermint tea helped.''

"I—okay.''

Ross climbed the stairs, assuring himself this was for the best. Hannah was too tempting, and he'd regret changing the conditions of their marriage.

That is, *if* she wanted to change them, he reflected. Maybe she didn't.

The thought was unreasonably depressing and he sank to the mattress, a dull ache in his temples. Perhaps he was actually getting a headache as punishment for his behavior.

A few minutes later Hannah appeared at the doorway with a steaming cup in hand. Ross looked at her from under his eyelids and groaned. The reasons for keeping things on a platonic level had never seemed less important. In fact, they seemed downright stupid.

"Ross?'' Hannah murmured. When he didn't move, she set the cup on the bedstead and turned as if to leave.

His hand shot out and caught her wrist. "Don't.''

Her eyes widened. "Don't what?''

"Leave.'' His voice was low and guttural with suppressed need.

Hannah's breathing quickened as Ross's thumb stroked her pulse point. He drew her closer until she sat next to him on the bed, all the while watching her with a feral intensity.

"A massage might help,'' he murmured. Slowly he put her hands on his chest.

"I didn't realize migraine treatment required a massage…here.'' The muscular pads beneath her palms were hard with tension.

"You know perfectly well I don't have a migraine."

"Do I?" She smiled as his fingers grasped her waist, a wordless growl coming from his lips. She heard that growl a lot, especially when Ross was frustrated.

Her lashes swept downward, concealing the path of her gaze. Below his belt there was an awesome bulge, and the sight sent a flutter of nerves through her tummy. It was difficult imagining the two of them...*fitting* together.

"If it was that bad, the human race would have ended a long time ago," Ross said quietly.

A blush burned her cheeks. Apparently she hadn't been successful in hiding her thoughts, *or* the direction she was looking. "I never thought it would be bad."

His hands inched upward until they cupped her breasts. "Really?"

"Really." Her breath rushed out as he teased her nipples into taut peaks. "I just wondered about the logistics. I know where all the parts go."

"And why...?"

"I have a pretty good idea about the 'why' part, too." Hannah gasped as Ross spun her across his body. She landed on the mattress with a surprised squeak. "Ross?"

"I can't fight it anymore," he said grimly. "If you don't want to consummate our marriage, say so now."

Her mouth pressed together. She had no intention of saying anything so foolish.

"Are you sure, Hannah?"

With the tip of her finger she traced the firm line of his jaw and measured the purpose in his eyes. Pain and doubt lingered behind that purpose, but the decision was made for both of them; she couldn't turn away, any more than she could stop breathing.

"I'm sure."

"Good."

The tension eased in Ross's chest and he brushed shining strands of hair from Hannah's face. She was so beautiful. He'd always loved her eyes, so changeable, like the silver mist swirling across a hemlock forest.

"I want to see you," he whispered. "*All* of you."

Pink flags adorned her cheeks again, but she didn't protest when he pulled her to her feet and eased the negligee from her shoulders. He ran his fingers down the slippery silk of the nightgown until he pressed them on her abdomen, just above the shadowed triangle that hid her feminine secrets. Her muscles tightened beneath his touch and he dragged air into his lungs.

Hannah's womb.

The blood in his groin pooled hot and heavy. She'd consented to sleeping with him, but not necessarily to having a child. Ross fought to think through the thick heat in his veins. He could protect Hannah from pregnancy—*should* protect her. A baby would be a complication they couldn't handle.

Slowly, still giving her time to protest, he untied the ribbons at each shoulder. Silk slithered downward, catching briefly on the aroused peaks of her breasts, then dropped to the floor. She did nothing to hide herself, the only reaction a deepening of color in her cheeks.

She was small—quite the smallest woman he'd ever held—yet there was nothing childlike about her body.

Slim, but perfectly formed, with a womanly roundness that pleased the eye and tempted the hands.

"Honeycomb..." Ross sighed. "I had no idea."

He lifted her in his arms and laid her on the tumbled pillows. For an instant he stepped back and gazed his fill. The delicate, exquisite woman gracing his bed was still a stranger. Her pale skin gleamed like a luminescent pearl in the softly lighted room. How could he have ever imagined Hannah was sturdy?

Self-protection.

Undoubtedly. It was so much safer not to acknowledge the beauty beneath her practical clothing. And she was so fragile. His own mother had died because she wasn't strong enough to survive the harsher climate of the north. But Hannah... He tensed, a new fear clutching his chest. Hannah was stronger than she looked. She *had* to be.

He couldn't lose her.

He pushed the unreasoned fear into the back of his mind, not wanting to examine its dimensions. Things were different now, with better medical care. And he could provide luxuries to make Hannah's life easier than that of his barely remembered mother.

"Ross?" The color in her eyes shifted. "Is something wrong with...me?" Her lashes swept down and she drew her arm across her body and he swore silently, never intending to make her feel vulnerable or inadequate.

"You're perfect." He tugged her arm away and covered one of her breasts with his hand. The eager nipple pressed into his palm and he groaned. "You just look so breakable," he confessed. "I'm afraid to touch you."

"I'm stronger than I look," Hannah said, a feminine smile tugging at her lips. She rose on her knees. "But it's your turn, now."

Her small hands tugged his shirttails from his jeans, then slid upward, under the fabric. The heated imprint of her fingers tore the breath from his throat.

"Don't you like this?" she asked, eyes closed as she concentrated on the flat disks of his nipples.

"Too damn much." Ross tore the shirt away himself, loath to forego the gentle caresses for even a moment. His jeans disappeared with equal speed until the only garment he wore was his underwear.

She looked at him with a questioning expression and he waited. He needed her to take the final step, to be certain she knew what she wanted. His head was muddled with half-formed notions about virgins, probably all wrong. But he couldn't bear to look in her eyes later and see regret for this night.

His own regrets would be enough.

"Ross?"

"Go ahead."

Hannah wasn't so innocent she didn't know what a naked man looked like, but a fully aroused male was certainly something new. She wet her lips with the edge of her tongue. There was a tense, waiting quality in Ross's silence and she guessed what he expected her to do.

Swallowing, she peeled the cotton away and down his powerful legs. What she saw took her breath away.

"Still sure?" he asked.

Hannah put her hand on Ross's chest and leaned fully against him, tearing a rasping groan from her husband. Her confidence was growing, driven by need and the certainty of how much he wanted her.

"Ah...Honeycomb," Ross muttered. He put one knee on the bed and swung them onto the mattress.

Her breath caught for an instant. He was so tall, he dwarfed her in the bed, his chest and shoulders so broad, he blocked everything from her sight... everything but him. It was intimidating, but she couldn't let it worry her. Ross might be bitter about love, but he was a good, decent man.

Ross stroked his wife, his fingers testing and finding the places she enjoyed being touched the most, delighting in the silken dew of her skin.

When they were both gasping for breath, he sheathed himself with a condom, then eased himself between her thighs. The knowledge that his act would change their relationship forever still throbbed in his brain, but it was a pale shadow to the desire that had taken control.

He moved carefully, shallowly, and she tensed.

"Easy, Honeycomb."

The childhood nickname should have cooled his blood, but instead it seemed a fitting endearment for the bedroom. Honey, from his honeycomb.

"Open your mouth, let me kiss you." He kissed her deeply and stroked her breasts again and again, building the sweet tension in both of them.

Let me do this right, he prayed.

As easily, gently as possible, he eased into Hannah's sweet warmth, absorbing her faint quiver of discomfort as if it were his own.

"I'm sorry," he whispered. "I hate hurting you."

"No. It's all right. It's better already."

Ross raised his head to look in her face, even as she relaxed beneath him. He knew how generous Hannah was; he wanted to be certain. "We could stop," he offered, hoping it was true and that his body wouldn't betray his better instincts.

Her husky laugh made his pulse leap. "Ross McCoy, if you stop, I'm going to kill you. Now, are you going to make love to me or not?"

He kissed her throat, already sensing the feminine contractions of her desire. Praying now for the self-control to hold his own need in check, he began to move, her supple warmth yielding to him without hesitation or sign of pain.

Hannah gasped as waves of passion tightened her body, splintering rational thought like the splintering of winter ice in the spring.

When she'd dreamed of making love, she'd imagined something softly romantic, a slow unraveling of the senses. But there was nothing slow or soft about it.

There was only Ross.

And finally only the fulfillment that exploded through them.

Ross stared at the ceiling, his mind an active contrast to the relaxed, sated condition of his body.

He'd made love to Hannah.

She lay asleep in his arms, her slight weight molded against him. He didn't know whether to rejoice or be scared out of his wits; his history with women didn't inspire him to confidence.

It was almost dawn, the eastern sky showing a slight rosiness on the horizon. The day would soon begin, along with the complications of the decision he'd made the evening before.

Hannah stirred, snuggling even closer, and the body he'd thought was satisfied leapt into attention.

"What am I going to do?" Ross whispered, delving his fingers through her hair. It flowed like cool, dry silk on his chest. Pretty, though not because of the haircut. He'd thought Hannah's hair was pretty before she fancied it up.

The subtle changes in breathing told him she was waking, and he tried to think of something to say. But all he wanted was to sweep her beneath him again, as he had more than once during the long hours of the night.

"Mmm." She stretched languidly. "Hello."

"Hello."

Hannah wiggled until she could look into Ross's face. He seemed distant, but there were ways to change that. Weren't there? "What time is it?"

"Uh...morning."

She gave him a fuzzy, happy smile. "Have you heard anything from Jamie's room?"

Ross glanced at the baby monitor on the bedside table and shook his head. "No. All quiet."

"He doesn't usually get up this early." Hannah traced the dark wedge of hair on Ross's chest, following the narrowing line until it disappeared above his waist. She ached, but it was a deliciously sensual ache. Her husband was a demanding lover and she'd loved every minute.

He cleared his throat. "I don't have to fly today, but I have some maintenance to do on the planes."

"Of course." Her hand drifted lower and he let out a strangled sound.

"Hannah, we can't. You must be uncomfortable after all those...times. A woman needs to recover after having sex for the first time. I should have remembered."

Sex?

In the back of Hannah's head she thought about correcting him. They weren't having sex, they were making love, and it was wonderful.

"I'm fine." She kissed the hard point of his nipple.

"I hope to hell you're telling the truth." Abruptly Ross rolled her over, and in a single thrust filled her to overflowing. Her initial gasp was lost in the hard pressure of his mouth, his tongue delving deeply, mirroring the same swift taking.

She drew her knees up, lost in the sensation of being desired so fiercely. Once, during the night, she'd worried about the sensual power Ross held over her. But there wasn't any use worrying, and it was nearly certain she shared a measure of that same power.

Much later, Hannah bent to straighten the rumpled bed. A small smear of blood stained the sheets and she smiled faintly at the evidence of their lovemaking.

Ross came to help, yet he paused when he saw the same red mark on the sheet. "I'm sorry," he whispered.

She turned and gave him a lingering kiss. "There's nothing to be sorry about. I quite...*enjoyed* the evening."

His eyebrows lifted. "And the morning?"

Hannah laughed. "That, too."

"Jamie is awake." Ross stared into her face, his eyes dark with undefined emotion.

She shifted uncomfortably, wondering what was going through his head. "I guess we'll have to talk later."

He frowned. "Talk? I think everything's been discussed."

"Ross, we need to—"

"No. Let's just leave it alone. I'll see you tonight."

Hannah accepted her husband's polite kiss and watched him leave. When the front door closed she sat on the bed and clutched a pillow to her chest. Making love with Ross was overwhelming—the most extraordinary thing she'd ever known—but doubt was creeping into her heart.

A new hairdo and clothing didn't solve problems, and neither did incredible sex. And it *was* just sex to Ross, not making love—that much was plain.

"Are you okay, Mommy?"

She looked up and smiled through her inner turmoil. Jamie sat just outside the bedroom door, petting Doggit. Yet there was a familiar worried expression on his face, and her own smile faded. He was more sensitive than other children, probably because of the way his mother had dragged him around.

"I'm fine, Jamie." Hannah held out her arms and he ran to her for a hug. She kissed the top of his head. "Your papa and I ate before you got up, but I'll fix you some breakfast after I make the bed."

"Cin'mon rolls?" he asked hopefully.

She ruffled his hair. "We can't have cinnamon rolls every morning, but I think there are some left. Go play for a while and I'll call you when the food is ready."

He gave her another hug and trotted out of the room. Thankfully his worries could often be pushed away by kisses and sweet rolls. If only her own worries could be handled as simply.

Talk? I think everything's been discussed.

Her mouth tightened. Ross was a master at avoiding discussion about important things. Nothing had really changed between them. They'd enjoyed hot sex together, that's all. Essentially, she was still a live-in housekeeper, with the added "fringe benefit" of sleeping with the boss.

Hannah pulled the stained sheets from the bed and threw them down the laundry chute. Of course, most women didn't have bosses who were so strong and gorgeous. The boy she'd known had grown into a wonderful man, but he didn't really want *her*.

In the mirror she saw her styled hair and her close-fitting sweater and wool skirt. The reflection didn't please her nearly as much as when she first got dressed. At most, Ross had responded to the clothing and other outward changes she'd made in herself.

Outward changes.

She'd done everything she knew to seduce him. He'd probably make love to any woman in the same circumstances.

"And why not?" Hannah fumed.

Ross now had the perfect world—a housekeeper, baby-sitter and cozy bed partner, all without the dangerous complications of being in love. Obviously physical intimacy didn't translate to emotional closeness. Their childhood friendship should have made them close, but she felt further apart from him than ever.

"Well, fine," she muttered. "He wants a baby-sitter and housekeeper. So that's *all* he gets until he figures out what's really important."

She swiftly made up the bed, determined to remove all evidence of her presence from the room. The last thing she took was the forgotten cup from the table by the bed, yet tears spilled down her cheeks as she poured the cold peppermint tea down the bathroom drain.

Perhaps Ross was right; she needed recovery time. Only, it wasn't her body that needed to heal, it was her heart.

The house was quiet when Ross let himself in. An unexpected flight had come up when a Triple M pilot was delayed by a storm in the Arctic. Ross had called Hannah to say he'd be later than expected, and the memory of her subdued response had distracted him for hours.

The murmur of voices from the second floor drew him and he paused at the door of the playroom, watching Hannah and Jamie together. His son was already in pajamas, his fresh-scrubbed face blinking sleepily.

"But how *does* water makes steam?" he asked, plainly asking a question he'd already posed more than once.

"It gets warm and expands," Hannah explained, using her hands to demonstrate. "Teeny bits of water moving so fast and hitting each other that they jump into the air."

Jamie didn't look convinced. "They jump like Doggit? Water doesn't have legs."

She laughed softly. "No, it doesn't."

"Hey, Tiger," Ross said.

"Papa!" Jamie charged over and Ross swung him high in his arms. "Me and Mommy made pizza today. Did you know you can make pizza? It doesn't have to come in a box."

Ross cleared his throat uncomfortably. They'd eaten plenty of restaurant pizza before Hannah became a part of their lives. "Yeah, I know."

"I like Mommy's best."

"Your mother does everything well." He glanced

at Hannah, a sensual smile on his lips, but she brushed past him without meeting his gaze. His brow creased in a frown.

"Time for bed, Jamie," she called over her shoulder.

"Can I play with Papa?"

"For a little while," she agreed.

"I'll be right there, Tiger." Ross put his son down and followed Hannah. "Uh…what you said about steam was great, even if he didn't believe it."

She bent and picked up a toy left on the floor. "Jamie wouldn't understand molecules and kinetic energy."

"Kinetic energy? I didn't know you were so familiar with physics." He gave her a teasing smile, despite an uneasy sensation growing in his chest. This wasn't the same Hannah he'd left in the morning; she was acting completely opposite.

"Quicksilver isn't the end of the world. I've taken dozens of mail-order courses. I have a college degree and everything."

"I didn't mean…" Ross's words trailed off—he might as well ask because he wasn't getting anywhere with diplomacy. "Hell, Hannah. What's wrong?"

"Nothing." She looked at him coolly.

"That isn't true. Are you angry because I had to go to work after—" he hesitated "—after we slept together?"

"I'm not angry at all."

He scowled as Hannah turned and disappeared down the stairs. Just that morning he'd held a warm and beguiling wife in his arms, and now he was in danger of getting frostbite.

Women. They were impossible.

After a few minutes of play, Jamie got sleepy again and Ross tucked him into bed without protest.

"I want Mommy to kiss me," the four-year-old said between wide yawns.

He wasn't the only one. Ross's greatest fears had come true; he was fast becoming obsessed with Hannah. He'd spent the day in a permanent state of semi-arousal. He needed Hannah more than he ever wanted to need anyone, a need that had nothing to do with providing a mother for his son. In fact, it wasn't even entirely about sex.

"I'll tell her," Ross whispered. "Now close your eyes and try to sleep."

"Not till Mommy comes." Jamie's tone was stubborn.

Ross sighed and went downstairs. He found Hannah in the kitchen, and she pulled a steaming plate from the microwave when she saw him.

"Jamie wants a kiss," he told her. "He says he won't go to sleep until you come."

She nodded and wiped her hands on a towel. "All right. There's more food in the refrigerator if that isn't enough to fill you up. Good night."

Good night?

Nine o'clock and she was saying good night?

His appetite vanishing, Ross grabbed a beer from the fridge and slugged it down. Hannah had acted normally around Jamie, but he was definitely getting the cold shoulder. Not that it necessarily meant something. Woman had odd turns of mood; even Mike's wife was prone to peculiar behavior.

Well, he'd just wait until she came down again and they could talk things out.

A short, humorless laugh came from Ross's throat

when he remembered that *he* was the one who'd avoided any discussion with Hannah. He'd refused to discuss their kiss in front of the fire, and this morning he'd said they didn't have anything to talk about. *After sleeping together.* After the best night of his life.

He groaned, mentally kicking himself. Perhaps she was angry, thinking he'd dismissed the importance of them becoming intimate.

Angry enough to leave?

Ross's skin went cold at the unbidden thought. His first wife had walked out without warning. But Hannah wasn't like Doreen, was she?

Chapter Ten

Don't borrow trouble.

The old saying wasn't any comfort, but Ross didn't have a choice except to wait for Hannah's return.

They would have to talk. It was slowly sinking into his brain that his marriage plan had a few flaws. Actually, the "plan" had so many holes, it was a wonder she'd married him in the first place.

Hannah could do anything she wanted; why would she stay in a marriage that didn't give her what she deserved?

Pain lanced through his head, the beginnings of a genuine migraine. He was sick at the idea of losing Hannah, but he wasn't sure what she wanted, and whether he could give her what she wanted even if he did know.

Her bedroom door closed, the sound barely discernible in the quiet house. She'd apparently slipped down the hall, avoiding the kitchen.

Ross's eyes narrowed. She didn't want to talk with

him? It was illogical, but he was furious. Hannah was
his wife. He wouldn't let her leave him without fighting it every step of the way.

"Hannah?" He knocked on her door. "We need to
talk."

Inside the bedroom Hannah rolled her eyes. *Now* he
wanted to talk? He should be happy she wanted to be
alone, it made his life so much easier. No complications. No need to get his heart involved.

"Hannah?"

"I'm tired, Ross."

He turned the knob and walked right in. Hannah
glared and jumped up from the bed. "What are you
doing?"

"Talking to my wife. I want to know what happened in the last twelve hours to make you act like
this."

"Nothing happened." She turned her back so he
wouldn't see the tears that threatened her composure.
"I don't know what you mean."

"Right. Everything is just peachy," Ross said sar-
castically. "We slept together last night. Do you regret
it? Is that the problem?"

Hannah drew a shaky breath. "I just need some
recovery time. That *is* what you suggested this morning, isn't it?"

She jumped as Ross's hands settled on her shoulders, rubbing up and down her arms in a soothing
motion. "I'm sorry, Honeycomb. I should have realized—this is all new to you, isn't it?"

He kissed the curve of her neck and a traitorous
shaft of response went through her body. She swallowed and lifted her chin. Ross might be able to cajole
her into relenting, but she couldn't let him. Not if she

wanted them to have a real future, including more children and laughter and shared worries and joys.

"Don't play the superior male, all knowing about his innocent little bride," she snapped.

"That isn't it at all." The hands stroking her arms hesitated. "I'm just trying to understand. We're married, we have to communicate."

"Don't you see?" Hannah whirled and poked her finger in his chest. "You decide when we talk, and when we don't. That isn't a marriage, it isn't even a friendship. Now get out of my room."

Ross set his jaw. "No. You're my wife."

"Ha."

"What is that supposed to mean?"

"It means you know less about being married than you know about women, and you know pretty darned little about women!"

His eyes darkened dangerously. "You're not making any sense. All right, I admit that it was crazy to think we could live together and not have sex. We're both healthy adults who have certain needs."

"That's all it is to you—needs. Just sex." Hannah pressed her hand on her tummy. She was shaking so hard, she could hardly stand. "Feelings have nothing to do with it."

"Hannah…we aren't lovesick kids. We can work things out without tearing each other apart. I know what that's like, because I *have* been in love."

An icy calm descended on Hannah. "Love isn't something that destroys you. You didn't love Doreen, you *wanted* her, the way a child wants a toy. She was sexy and beautiful and your body did the thinking. Then you conveniently blamed your out-of-control hormones on love."

"That isn't true."

"Yes, it is." She swept the tears from her cheeks. "I know what love is. My parents were in love—passionately and completely. I want a husband loves me, not a man who just satisfies my needs."

"Just satisfies?" He stiffened, outraged pride in every line of his body. "Is that what you call last night? Satisfying?"

"It was wonderful," Hannah admitted. "But that was before I realized it didn't mean a darn thing."

Ross had trouble breathing, as though he'd been struck in the stomach with a massive fist. "You're leaving then?"

Hannah shook her head. "Of course not. But until you figure out what a marriage is really supposed to be, you can forget about traditional marital comforts. Believe it or not, Ross McCoy, love and lust are two entirely different things. If you can't understand that, then you aren't half the man I thought you were. Now get out of my room."

Stunned, Ross stared at Hannah, his thoughts in turmoil. What did she mean, love and lust? Was she implying she'd fallen in love with him?

"Go." She pointed to the door. "I'm not kidding, Ross. As of right now, you're getting the marriage you wanted. And you know what they say, don't you?" Her face was white with both pain and anger.

"What?"

"Be careful what you ask for, because you just might get it!"

Ross spent the night sitting in Jamie's bedroom, watching his son sleep.

"I hope you make better choices than your old

man,'' he whispered as dawn filled the windows with light. "Pick a woman like Hannah in the first place."

Ross leaned forward and massaged the back of his neck. A brutal headache had faded after taking a prescription painkiller, but the strong medication couldn't cure the confusion in his mind.

"What a royal mess," he murmured.

In one hand he held the baby monitor, the volume turned down to keep from disturbing Hannah. Neither of them had gotten a great deal of rest the previous night. He wanted her to sleep as long as possible.

Sleep... He smiled bitterly. If only *he* could sleep. One night of loving Hannah and he couldn't face his own bedroom.

You didn't love Doreen, you wanted her.

Love and lust are two entirely different things. If you can't understand that, then you aren't half the man I thought you were....

Did Hannah love him? For all her ability to cook and clean and bring order to chaos, she was a dreamer. He'd known that when he married her. But he hadn't truly seen the beautiful, passionate woman she'd become. Could she sleep with a man unless she loved him?

Another hour and a half passed while he wrestled with the question in his heart, torn between a distrust of love, and the fear of losing his Honeycomb.

The ring of the doorbell through the quiet house was a welcome relief. Jamie stirred sleepily, then curled up again. Ross slipped out and started down the stairs.

Hannah was ahead of him, but she barely flicked a glance in his direction as she opened the door.

"Who the hell are you?" demanded an ominously familiar voice.

Ross uttered a silent curse and descended the remaining steps in a rush.

"I'm Hannah McCoy," Hannah said evenly, staring at the woman on her doorstep. It didn't take a great deal of guesswork to figure out *her* identity.

Doreen.

The ex-wife from hell. Despite what she'd learned of the woman's character, Hannah could see why Ross had flipped over her. A tall, extremely well-endowed redhead—definitely not her natural color—with a smoldering sexiness that shrieked "Jump me." She was rather obvious, but men seemed to like that kind of thing.

"Hannah McCoy?" Doreen repeated. "What are you, Ross's sister?"

"No, I happen to be his wife," Hannah said, keeping a firm grasp on her temper *and* the door. She had no intention of letting the other woman into the house.

"Wife?" The news obviously came as an unwelcome surprise.

"What are you doing here, Doreen?" Ross asked in a lethal tone. He put his hands on Hannah's shoulders, backing her up, and she could sense the anger radiating through him.

"I want to see the kid."

"You agreed to stay away."

Doreen's smile turned sly. "You can't keep me from my son." Ross apparently had the same idea about keeping his ex-wife outside, because he nudged Hannah through the door and closed it sharply behind them.

"Think again. Jamie's been messed up enough by your irresponsible lifestyle."

Doreen lit a cigarette and took a long drag of smoke.

"A judge might think differently. And it's your word against mine. I could claim your new little wifey-dear messed him up."

"You vile—"

"Don't." Hannah grabbed Ross's arm as he took hasty steps toward his ex-wife. He wasn't a violent man, but Doreen might try to claim he'd intimidated her.

"Keep your mouth shut about Hannah," Ross ordered. "You aren't fit to be in the same borough with her."

"Borough?" Their unwelcome visitor took another long drag on her cigarette. "That's part of this godforsaken state's quaint governmental system, right?"

Hannah's dislike for the other woman was growing in leaps and bounds. She loved Alaska and she loved her family, and she wouldn't let anyone hurt them. "Our 'system' is none of your business," she said sharply. "Jamie is in a stable home and Ross has custody. You can't do anything to change that."

Doreen shrugged, unperturbed. "Custody battles are so ugly. And expensive, even if you win. Now if I were to receive a generous sum of money as compensation for the loss of my parental rights, I might be convinced not to go to court."

"I already paid you a fortune," Ross snarled.

"Ross, *darling,*" Doreen mocked. "You paid me some money, but hardly a fortune."

"How dare you?" Hannah said, shaking with fury. The woman wanted money? Most people would thanks their lucky stars to have a son like Jamie, and this…this *person* only wanted to use him for her own selfish gains.

"I'm his mother. I can 'dare' anything I want."

Ross clenched his jaw so hard it hurt. How could he have ever been attracted to Doreen? Worse, how could he have been so blind about her character? Hannah was right, his body had done his thinking. He'd never loved Doreen, he'd just wanted her.

"I know all about you," Hannah said fiercely. "You're a selfish, mercenary witch with the morals of an alley cat. You aren't getting your claws into Jamie again. *Ever.* You've exploited him for the last time."

Doreen's mouth opened, but she didn't have a chance to say anything.

"Jamie has one mother, and her name is Hannah McCoy," Hannah continued in a quieter tone, but no one could miss the deadly intent of her words. "If anyone tries to take him away, they'll regret ever hearing of Alaska."

Ross let out a low whistle, remembering the night he'd convinced her to marry him. She'd reminded him of a mama cougar, protecting her young, but that was nothing compared to the claws she was flexing now.

"You neglected Jamie to the point of child abuse, and I would take great pleasure in seeing you arrested for it." Hannah pointed to Doreen's car. "Now get out of Alaska before we *do* call the state troopers…who, I might add, will be very sympathetic to our point of view."

Doreen swallowed visibly. She'd met her match and she knew it. After a moment, she shrugged her shoulders and tossed her cigarette on the ground.

"Fine. Keep the little brat. I don't really need the money anyway." She hurried to her car, somewhat faster than Ross had ever seen her move, and roared away from the house.

"Good riddance," Hannah muttered.

"She does outstay her welcome."

Ross wanted to grab Hannah and whirl her around and around, rejoicing in their victory. And he had no question in his mind it was a victory. For all her grasping nature, Doreen wasn't a fool; she knew when the odds were against her. At heart, he suspected she was a coward, afraid of taking responsibility for her life, and certainly too afraid to deal with Hannah.

He looked at his wife, but she had already turned toward the house. "Hannah?"

"I'll check on Jamie, then get breakfast," she said evenly, all emotion wiped from her voice.

The memory of their argument returned in full force and Ross sighed. Seeing his ex-wife again brought everything into focus. The two women were as different as night and day—Hannah was all the wonderful things Doreen wasn't. She'd never leave; she was the kind of woman who kept a promise to her dying day.

A squirrel wandered by, its eyes blinking sleepily. Something had kept him awake into daylight, perhaps the rigors of feeding himself for the winter.

"Lucky for you that Doggit is an inside cat," Ross murmured.

The squirrel flipped its tailed and disappeared into the forest.

Ross rubbed his temples, his head fogged by lack of sleep. He'd forgotten how much he trusted Hannah, the very trust that made him propose in the first place. She'd promised to become Jamie's mother and she'd keep that promise, no matter how much her stubborn husband acted like a jackass.

Hmm. A smile grew on his face. Thinking of Hannah as his wife had come with surprising ease, but now he loved the sound of that *other* word—*husband.*

He loved her. Wholly and completely.

It was as simple as that. Love might be a risk, but losing her was unthinkable. Hannah had stolen his heart with each shy blush and perceptive insight. She'd woven herself into his life so completely, he couldn't drink a cup of coffee or climb into a plane without needing to be with her.

"Can't really blame her for being upset with me," Ross murmured.

He sat on the step, deep in thought. He wanted to be Hannah's husband in every sense of the word. Only, they should have a new start to their marriage, something fresh to put the past behind them.

He'd regretted their hasty wedding in Nevada, though it would be something to laugh about with their children and grandchildren. But Hannah's dreams of getting married in Quicksilver could still come true. He wanted to give her the world, and a romantic white wedding seemed a good place to start. Something special, a surprise planned with the help of his friends and her father.

Yup. A simple apology probably wouldn't convince Hannah he'd changed. And she was still too angry to listen properly. A couple of days would help cool her temper. Then he could spring the wedding on her.

To win his case, he needed something special, just like the woman he loved.

"Airsick, Honeycomb?"

"No." Hannah looked out the window of the plane. Over the past three days since Doreen's appearance, Ross had been solicitous of her health, affectionate and attentive. In other words, he'd totally ignored her attempts to stay aloof and detached.

The rat.

And now they were flying to Quicksilver with a microwave, chest freezer and load of high-quality convenience foods packed into the cargo section of the plane. For her father, Ross had explained that morning before leaving.

A part of her was beginning to unravel—the part that was so certain about making Ross fall in love with her. Was it fair? They'd gotten married with certain expectations, and now she wanted something more.

Hannah crossed her arms over her stomach and slumped deeper into her seat. Maybe she was pregnant from that night they'd spent together and it would make Ross confront the way he felt. He hadn't used any protection the last two times they'd made love. Heck, she came from a fertile family— obviously her mother never had trouble getting pregnant.

No. Hannah shook her head. Biology wouldn't be that kind. Besides, it hadn't been the right time of the month for her.

Edgar Liggett was waiting at the airstrip for them, though he pointedly avoided looking at the plane until it had come to a complete stop.

"Hi, Dad." Hannah swallowed back tears as he lifted her in a huge bear hug.

"You look good," Edgar said when he put her down. He touched her hair, then glanced at her stylish black denim jeans and white cable-knit sweater. "Different, though."

She shrugged. "Not that different."

Her father smiled kindly. "That's right. Let's go back to the house and visit. It seems like you've been gone forever."

"Hello, Edgar." Ross held out his hand and the two

men shook. "We brought a few things for the house, so we need to unload the plane first."

The two men worked companionably while she held Jamie. He wanted to help, but even the food was too heavy for a four-year-old to lift, being packed in coolers with dry ice to keep it frozen.

As they approached the house, her father cleared his throat nervously. "I didn't expect you to come so soon...so uh, there's a small problem about sleeping arrangements."

The back of Hannah's neck prickled in warning. "What kind of problem?"

"You know those old beds? The mattresses were all broken-down and such. You've been after me for years to replace them, so I decided to pitch the old stuff."

Hannah closed her eyes and prayed she wasn't going to hear what she knew was coming. "Yes?"

"I kept my old bed until a new one came, and that one in your room, but the rest got burned."

Oh, God.

"But it's all right," Edgar assured. "Jamie can bunk with me, and the two of you can sleep in your old room."

She looked accusingly at Ross, but he just lifted his shoulders.

"Sounds fine, Edgar," Ross drawled. "But if I'd known, I could have brought a couple new beds in the Beaver. Its got a huge payload capacity."

"That so? Haven't paid much attention to flying since...well, for a long time. But I hear it's a damn good plane. A real workhorse."

Hannah dropped her face against the back of Jamie's head while her husband and father discussed the relative merits of planes used in the frontier state. This wasn't happening. She wasn't going to sleep in the same bed with Ross; it was a terrible nightmare that would go away when she woke up.

Or maybe it wouldn't.

She snuck a peak at Ross and wondered if her resolve was strong enough to spend the night next to him without attacking the man.

Maybe he didn't have to love her. Maybe extreme *like* was good enough. Hannah moaned.

Maybe she'd lost her marbles.

Hours later Hannah was convinced that something fishy was going on between her father and Ross. They seemed entirely too cordial and friendly.

"Something is up, and I want to know what it is," she said once they were alone in her childhood bedroom.

Ross unbuttoned his shirt. "What do you think could be up?"

Hannah hesitated. "You went right along with Dad's suggestion about the arrangements for tonight. You didn't object to us sleeping...in the same bed."

"Nope." His smile was extremely annoying, mostly because it made shivers go through her stomach. "I'd never object to that, Honeycomb."

"You did once," she said desperately. "Remember? When we talked that first night over hot chocolate, you said we wouldn't be intimate."

"As I recall, I said we'd have to get reacquainted and make a decision later. Seems to me, the decision's been made."

She glared. "You can't possibly imagine I'm going to sleep with you."

Ross tossed his shirt on a chair and unzipped his jeans. "Sleep, yes. Make love, no."

"What do you think you're doing?" Hannah yelped as he hooked his thumbs into the elastic of his underwear and tugged.

"Getting ready for bed, dear wife. I sleep in the nude."

The underwear went down and Hannah spun around, turning her back on his male glory. "You can just put that back on."

A soft thud came from the corner of the room. "Don't want to." There was a rustling of blankets and the bed creaked beneath his weight. "I'm tired and need some rest. Anyway, the walls are too thin to make love properly. You aren't exactly quiet when we get going."

"You...argh!" Hannah looked at him again, hardly able to speak, both from anger and embarrassment. "That's a despicable thing to say."

Ross put his hands behind his head and grinned. "No, it's not. It's the sort of thing lovers talk about, though usually with less space between them." He pulled one hand out and patted the covers next to him. "Come to bed, Honeycomb. I won't bite, but I would like a good-night kiss."

"Forget it."

Tingling from head to toe with the heat of his eyes, Hannah grabbed her nightgown and fled to the bathroom to change. She didn't have a great deal of choice about the sleeping arrangements, but she'd be darned if she let him coax her into a kiss.

One kiss and she'd be a goner.

Heck, she could just sleep on the floor. Or on the sofa. She thought about it for a minute, then shook her head. You'd have to be a masochist to sleep on her father's sofa, and the floor was like ice. With Ross in the bed, she'd be warm and toasty all night.

And she'd be a lot warmer if she relented about this sex-without-love stuff. It might be worth thinking about. Most of her wrath had faded in the past couple days, and maintaining a distance was difficult without anger to bolster her resolve.

With as much dignity as she could muster, Hannah walked back into her bedroom. Ross was turned on his side, away from the middle of the bed, and he appeared to be asleep.

Her eyes narrowed. He'd gotten her all heated up and willing to negotiate, and now he was asleep without a care in the world.

Men were slime.

Chapter Eleven

Mmm, she was warm.

And comfortable.

Hannah yawned and looked down at the arms wrapped around her body. They were large and muscular and didn't belong to her.

"Ohmigod."

She was lying on her side, with Ross snuggled up behind her, spoon fashion. The thin silk of her nightgown was the only thing separating them, and from the heat pressed to her bottom, it obviously wasn't enough.

"What?" His voice rumbled through her.

"You…uhm…" Her words ended in a low moan as his thumb rubbed her nipple. Sensations skidded through her at light speed, turning every good intention she'd ever possessed into pure desire.

Drat him. She wanted to be strong. She'd tried to be grateful that he'd fallen sleep, but instead she'd wanted to scream. Now he was melting her sleepy senses with each lingering caress and she didn't have the strength to fight him. Maybe tomorrow, but not now.

"Don't, Ross." Yet even to her own ears, it was a halfhearted protest.

His hands drew the thin silk up her legs until he could stroke the bare curve of her hip. Hannah's fingers dug into the side of the mattress until they were numb.

"Don't what? Don't make love to my wife?"

"We aren't...I said we weren't going...*oh, dear.*"

Ross tugged his wife onto her back and dragged the hem of her gown higher. He hadn't planned to make love to Hannah until things were settled between them, but she was too tempting and he needed her too much.

"How did you stay a virgin all those years?" he whispered. "You're so passionate, so responsive. It boggles my mind."

"That's my concern." She was trying to sound nonchalant, but he knew better. The scent of her arousal was an aphrodisiac and he exulted that she responded to him so intensely. He surely had a chance if she could want him that much.

Leaning down, Ross kissed the soft curve of her belly. The muscles beneath his mouth rippled with tension and he blew softly. Perhaps she'd have their baby one day, and he would feel it moving beneath his hands and mouth. He wanted that with an urgent longing that both shocked and thrilled him.

For the past four years Jamie was the only thing he thought about. The idea of having another child never occurred to him, yet now it was something exciting and wonderful to consider.

"You'd be so beautiful with a baby inside you," he whispered.

Hannah desperately pulled air into her lungs.

A baby?

No, Ross didn't mean that. Men said things they didn't really mean when they were in bed. At least, that's what Ten Penny Alice always claimed. And Ten Penny ought to know something about men with all her experience.

Ross's hand massaged her abdomen and warmth invaded the space between Hannah's legs. Slowly he kissed his way up her body, his caresses pushing away the silk garment until he pulled it over her head and flung it to the floor.

"Good morning, Mrs. McCoy," he murmured.

She kept her hands at her side with a tremendous effort. The night they'd spent together, she'd lost herself in touching him, exploring his male textures so different from her own. There were natural curves and crevices between men and women that made them fit together perfectly.

Cupping Hannah's breasts, Ross rolled her nipples between his fingers, then kissed each velvet peak. He knew he ought to stop, but *knowing* and *doing* were two different things.

"Honeycomb," he breathed, drawing one taut peak between his lips and rubbing across the surface with his tongue. "You taste so sweet. I never imagined a woman could taste so sweet."

"We're all...the same."

"No, we were made for each other." Ross eased her legs apart, alert to any sign of resistance. "Shall I stop, Hannah?" He brushed her unprotected softness and she moaned.

"No."

Hannah gasped as Ross sank into her. He felt so good, so right.

"Still tender?" he murmured, his voice rumbling both through her and within her. She moaned at the shivering sensation, his thick presence within her body more necessary than the air she breathed.

"Don't stop. Don't ever stop."

He laughed and the sensations increased. Hannah dragged her nails across his shoulders and he shuddered, driving into her, all thoughts of teasing laughter forgotten.

Ripples of fulfillment caught them both and she bit her lip, trying to stay silent.

Sensing her struggle, Ross covered her mouth with a kiss and absorbed the ecstatic cries she couldn't suppress. And a moment after his pulsing release, her own body shattered with a thousand bursts of light.

Minutes later, Hannah floated back into herself, though random shudders still shook her body. Ross lay heavily on top of her, yet somehow his much greater weight didn't crush, it protected. He ran his hands over her, soothing her shivers with long, gentle strokes.

When the final quiver had faded, Hannah ached for another reason—the knowledge that they were still the same two people, at cross purposes with each other.

She wasn't angry any longer; the last dregs had vanished with their frantic loving. But she'd rather be angry. The anger had sustained her; now there was only sadness.

"I need to get up."

Ross gave her a gentle squeeze. "Okay."

Hannah pulled her nightgown over her head and hastily retreated to the bathroom to collect her thoughts. It felt so natural waking up with Ross and making love with him. But it didn't mean anything. She'd read about biological processes. She knew some men woke up aroused, and she'd been convenient.

That's right.

He'd gone to sleep on her the night before, so how much could he really want her? *Just* her?

We were made for each other. Hannah's knees wobbled at the memory of Ross's sensual claim, and she clutched the sink. But that was just about sex, wasn't it?

She pushed her hair back with her fingers and shook herself with a stern warning. Strangely, she'd slept quite well, unlike the past few nights. How could she fall asleep next to Ross, but not when she was alone? They'd only spent one other night together, so she couldn't have gotten into the habit of being with him.

The house was still quiet as she rinsed her face. The glass in the ancient mirror above the sink was chipped and wavy and she touched the reflection with her finger. Until a couple of weeks ago, she'd looked into that mirror every morning of her life…and until recently, she had usually had two or more brothers pounding on the door and demanding their turn in the bathroom.

She didn't mind the shabby condition of her childhood home, any more than she minded breathing, but this wasn't home any longer. Ross was home, whether they lived in his beautiful house or in a shack.

That's what her mother had known. Her mother had left the warmth of her darling South Carolina and come to a colder, wilder place because she loved a man. She'd fallen for a wounded soldier, recuperating from a terrible war, and left everything she knew to be with him.

"Oh, Ross," Hannah whispered. "We're in a real tangle."

Her heart aching, she walked back to the bedroom. The bed was empty except for a bouquet of long-stemmed red roses, lying on her pillow.

Roses?

She lifted the bouquet and inhaled the rich scent.

"Happy two-week anniversary," Ross said softly.

Hannah turned and looked at her husband, leaning against the door frame. He was dressed only in a pair of jeans and he made her breathless. She swallowed and focused on the roses.

"They're beautiful. Thank you."

"You're very welcome." Ross took a breath. This was it. The big moment, when he'd know if Hannah could forgive him for being so blind. He straightened and closed the door behind him. "I brought something special for you to wear today."

"Two-week anniversaries don't rate something special," she said dryly.

"I don't know.... You gave me a special anniversary present this morning, didn't you?"

Pink flagged her cheeks at the reminder and he grinned. He'd always treasure Hannah's sweet core of innocence.

"I have a surprise," he said. "I think you'll enjoy it."

"I don't know, I think I've had enough surprises." Hannah sat on the edge of the bed, stroking one of the velvet red buds he'd given her. "But what is it?"

He went to the closet and took out the gown he'd hung there just minutes before. It was the antique wedding dress that once belonged to Hannah's mother. He'd asked Callie to have it cleaned and pressed and sized to his wife's petite dimensions.

The flowers fell unnoticed to Hannah's feet, her eyes wide with shock. "What are you doing with my mother's wedding dress?"

"We're getting married."

She blinked. "We're already married."

He shook his head and walked toward her, tension coiling deep in his gut. "No. We're having a real white wedding in the church, with all our friends and your father giving you away, instead of a friendly cab-driver. Flowers, cake, photographers...the whole shooting match, just the way you always wanted."

Hannah stared, dumbfounded.

It was just like Ross, arranging things and assuming he knew best. He didn't ask, he just did what he thought was right without so much as a by-your-leave.

"That's ridiculous."

Eyes intent, he knelt in front of her. "There's nothing ridiculous about marrying the woman you love. Will you marry me, Hannah Liggett?"

Abruptly Hannah had a hard time breathing. She wanted to believe him. He was offering her everything she'd ever wanted, but it was like waking up in a dream, and she warned herself to be careful.

"You don't trust me. You don't trust love."

"I trusted you, I just didn't trust myself. But you taught me about love, Honeycomb. You were right. Love doesn't destroy, it makes you strong. It just took me a while to believe it."

Ross held out his hand and she saw a channel set diamond ring, identical to the one she'd secretly admired in Reno. And next to it, was a man's broad gold wedding band. She touched the plain gold ring with the tip of her finger, and Ross smiled a brilliant, heart-stopping smile.

"I love you," he said. "I want to start over...the right way."

Hannah searched his eyes and the expression glowing in them made her dizzy. Tears spilled down her cheeks as she slid off the bed and into his arms.

"I love you, too."

"God, Honeycomb. I've been so scared it was too late." Ross held her tightly, afraid he was going to cry himself. He finally let go enough to kiss her lips, a sweet exchange of love that held nothing back and promised everything.

The thunder of little feet came down the hall and a hand pounded on the door.

"Papa, Grandpa wants to know if it's okay now?"

Ross drew back and smiled into Hannah's eyes, one hand cupping her cheek. "Our son wants to know if it's okay now."

Hannah covered his hand with her own, feeling like she'd swallowed the sun. "Tell him it's perfect," she whispered.

Epilogue

Exactly two years later

Hannah lit the last candle and blew out the match.
Jamie was staying with the Fitzpatricks, the fire was
lit and Ross's favorite dinner was ready except for
the finishing touches.

She wanted their anniversary to be very, *very* special. Ross was determined not to celebrate the date
of their wedding in Reno, so they were observing
the day they'd exchanged vows in Quicksilver.

It had been a day to remember forever. Callie
Fitzpatrick's father was a pastor and he'd flown in
from Washington to conduct the ceremony. The
guests included everyone in Quicksilver, from Ten
Penny Alice and her husband to Hannah's brothers,
with the happy addition of Ross's partners and her
own father.

And everywhere there had been flowers and white

lace, and the most important part of all...the love between bride and groom.

A framed wedding picture sat on a table near the couch and Hannah lifted it, tears of happiness shining in her eyes. Ross had worn an elegant suit for the ceremony, but the jacket quickly landed on the back of a chair during the reception. He held Jamie on one arm, and she leaned against his chest, securely encompassed by his other arm. They smiled into each other's eyes with a secret message.

Carefully she set the frame down again. The day of the wedding had been unusually warm for September and golden light suffused the candid photo. They had dozens of pictures, but this was their favorite.

With a last glance around the living room, Hannah hurried back to the kitchen to check dinner. Ross hadn't wanted to work today of all days, but an emergency had spoiled his plans. He'd be hungry after flying for ten hours.

"Happy anniversary, Honeycomb," Ross murmured, surprising her.

Hannah turned and smiled. "You came in very quietly, Mr. McCoy. I didn't hear a thing."

He pulled his hand from behind his back and presented her with a dozen red roses. "That's because I wanted to surprise you."

"You *always* surprise me," she teased. "Especially this morning. You woke me up from the inside out."

A dull red stained his neck. "I guess I was a little urgent. You seemed to be over the flu and I thought..." He shrugged.

"I'm not complaining."

Ross grinned. He could still make Hannah blush, but she could turn the tables on him quite effectively. Everything about his marriage was perfect, except for the faint sadness that occasionally crept into her silver-green eyes. She wanted a baby, but they hadn't been able to conceive.

According to the doctors, there wasn't anything physically wrong with either of them. But they fell into a group of people who, for some reason, had trouble making a baby together.

He'd like having another child, but it was Hannah's heartache that mattered. In another month they were flying to San Francisco to consult a leading fertility specialist. Ross dreaded the trip. The potential treatments would be hard on Hannah, both physically and emotionally, but it was what she wanted.

"Uh...Mike and Callie and Donovan all send their anniversary greetings," Ross murmured as his wife stirred fettuccine noodles into Alfredo sauce. On the counter there were seasoned steaks ready for broiling, a crisp Caesar salad ready for tossing and a blueberry pie ready for eating.

His stomach rumbled. *Loudly.*

"Didn't you eat those sandwiches I sent?" Hannah teased.

"Some, but I picked Donovan up in Fairbanks and he forced me to share. Then the ingrate said to put more horseradish on the French bread next time. Can you believe that?"

"Yes, that's Donovan." Hannah laughed and shook her head. "I make meat loaf sandwiches the way *you* like them. Donovan will just have to get his own wife."

Ross stepped behind her and pulled her back

against his chest. "He could never get as lucky as I did."

"Flatterer."

"Just honest." He spun her to him for a hungry kiss, his hands sliding beneath her fuzzy sweater to stroke her silken curves. "Let's wait and have a late dinner," he whispered. "*Very* late."

She blinked dreamily. "All right. Shall we toast our anniversary first?"

Ross nodded. "In the bedroom."

Hannah reached out a languid arm and handed him a bottle. "Take it in. I'll get the glasses."

He frowned as he looked at the bottle. "Honeycomb, this isn't the champagne, it's sparkling cider. Where's that vintage bottle I got for tonight?"

"Sorry." She swayed forward, kissed his chest and gave him a very private caress. "But I won't be drinking champagne for a while."

The caress addled him so much, he couldn't breathe. "Uh...why not?"

"The baby wouldn't like it."

Ross dragged air into his oxygen-starved lungs. He could swear Hannah had said "baby."

"Honeycomb?"

She was smiling, crying and laughing, all at the same time. "The doctor called this afternoon. I didn't have the flu, I'm pregnant. I'm just one of those women who get morning sickness all day long."

"Oh, God," Ross breathed. He cupped her face between his hands, rejoicing at the unfettered happiness in Hannah's eyes. "Are you sure?"

"As they used to say, the rabbit died. We're definitely having a baby."

Hannah laughed again as Ross swept her in his arms and whirled her about the kitchen. She might have been the last unmarried woman in Quicksilver, but she'd gotten the most wonderful husband of them all.

*　*　*　*　*

Look for JODIE'S MAIL ORDER MAN,
book 3 of JULIANNA MORRIS'S
fun-filled series, BRIDAL FEVER!
Available in July 2000!

Look Who's Celebrating Our 20th Anniversary:

"Happy 20th birthday, Silhouette. You made the writing dream of hundreds of women a reality. You enabled us to give [women] the stories [they] wanted to read and helped us teach [them] about the power of love."

—*New York Times* bestselling author
Debbie Macomber

"I wish you continued success, Silhouette Books.... Thank you for giving me a chance to do what I love best in all the world."

—International bestselling author
Diana Palmer

"A visit to Silhouette is a guaranteed happy ending, a chance to touch magic for a little while.... It refreshes and revitalizes and makes us feel better.... I hope Silhouette goes on forever."

—Award-winning bestselling author
Marie Ferrarella

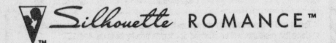

Silhouette ROMANCE™

Silhouette®

where love comes alive—online...

Visit the *Author's Alcove*

➤ Find the most complete information anywhere on your favorite Silhouette author.

➤ Try your hand in the Writing Round Robin— contribute a chapter to an online book in the making.

Enter the *Reading Room*

➤ Experience an interactive novel—help determine the fate of a story being created now by one of your favorite authors.

➤ Join one of our reading groups and discuss your favorite book.

Drop into *Shop eHarlequin*

➤ Find the latest releases—read an excerpt or write a review for this month's Silhouette top sellers.

➤ Try out our amazing search feature—tell us your favorite theme, setting or time period and we'll find a book that's perfect for you.

All this and more available at

www.eHarlequin.com
on Women.com Networks

SEYRB1